AROUND CHI-TOWN

March: We Chicagoans all live vicariously through our own "royalty," the Connelly family. And here comes a story to warm you up on a damp, blustery Chicago day....

Matriarch Emma Connelly has been keeping close tabs on what's going on in her island homeland of Altaria. The former princess has been in touch with her son, King Daniel, who tells her that a certain sheikh has been spending all his time in Altaria searching for a bride. And, says Daniel, he seems to have set his sights on the Connelly cousin Princess Catherine.

Having just lost her father and grandfather, and having been bypassed for the throne, the princess could use some good fortune. But sources close to her say not even the swarthy, sexy, studly sheikh is a match for the royal known around the globe as the Ice Princess.

Since the American king has taken the throne, Altaria has been making news with its peaceful transfer of power. But with the sparks flying between the sheikh and the princess. we're looking f to fireworks....

Dear Reader,

Celebrate the rites of spring with six new passionate, powerful and provocative love stories from Silhouette Desire!

Reader favorite Anne Marie Winston's *Billionaire Bachelors: Stone*, our March MAN OF THE MONTH, is a classic marriage-of-convenience story, in which an overpowering attraction threatens a platonic arrangement. And don't miss the third title in Desire's glamorous in-line continuity DYNASTIES: THE CONNELLYS, *The Sheikh Takes a Bride* by Caroline Cross, as sparks fly between a sexy-as-sin sheikh and a feisty princess.

In *Wild About a Texan* by Jan Hudson, the heroine falls for a playboy millionaire with a dark secret. *Her Lone Star Protector* by Peggy Moreland continues the TEXAS CATTLEMAN'S CLUB: THE LAST BACHELOR series, as an unlikely love blossoms between a florist and a jaded private eye.

A night of passion produces major complications for a doctor and the social worker now carrying his child in *Dr. Destiny*, the final title in Kristi Gold's miniseries MARRYING AN M.D. And an ex-marine who discovers he's heir to a royal throne must choose between his kingdom and the woman he loves in Kathryn Jensen's *The Secret Prince*.

Kick back, relax and treat yourself to all six of these sexy new Desire romances!

Enjoy!

Joan Marlow Golan

Joan Marlow Golan
Senior Editor, Silhouette Desire

Please address questions and book requests to:
Silhouette Reader Service
U.S.: 3010 Walden Ave., P.O. Box 1325, Buffalo, NY 14269
Canadian: P.O. Box 609, Fort Erie, Ont. L2A 5X3

The Sheikh
Takes a Bride
CAROLINE CROSS

Published by Silhouette Books
America's Publisher of Contemporary Romance

Special thanks and acknowledgment are given
to Caroline Cross for her contribution to
DYNASTIES: THE CONNELLYS series.

Special thanks to Ann Leslie Tuttle for suggesting me
for this story, Shannon Degen for patience above and beyond
the call of duty and Joan Marlow Golan for believing in me.
Silhouette Books is lucky to have you, and so am I.

 SILHOUETTE BOOKS

ISBN 0-373-76424-3

THE SHEIKH TAKES A BRIDE

Copyright © 2002 by Harlequin Books S.A.

Visit Silhouette at www.eHarlequin.com

Printed in U.S.A.

Books by Caroline Cross

Silhouette Desire

Dangerous #810
Rafferty's Angel #851
Truth or Dare #910
Operation Mommy #939
Gavin's Child #1013
The Baby Blizzard #1079
The Notorious Groom #1143
The Paternity Factor #1173
Cinderella's Tycoon #1238
The Rancher and the Nanny #1298
Husband—or Enemy? #1330
The Sheikh Takes a Bride #1424

CAROLINE CROSS

always loved to read, but it wasn't until she discovered romance that she felt compelled to write, fascinated by the chance to explore the positive power of love in people's lives. She grew up in Yakima, Washington, the "Apple Capital of the World," attended the University of Puget Sound and now lives outside Seattle, where she (tries to) work at home despite the chaos created by two telephone-addicted teenage daughters and a husband with a fondness for home-improvement projects. Pleased to have recently been #1 on a national bestseller list, she was thrilled to win the 1999 Romance Writers of America RITA Award for Best Short Contemporary Novel and to have been called "one of the best" writers of romance today by *Romantic Times*. Caroline believes in writing from the heart—and having a good brainstorming partner. She loves hearing from readers, and can be reached at P.O. Box 47375, Seattle, Washington 98146. Please include a SASE for reply.

MEET THE CONNELLYS

Meet the Connellys of Chicago—
wealthy, powerful and rocked by scandal,
betrayal...and passion!

Who's Who in *The Sheikh Takes a Bride*

Princess Catherine Rosemere—This Connelly cousin
doesn't believe in happily-ever-after—not even in her
storybook kingdom of Altaria. In this chapter of her life,
the last thing she needs is a sexy sheikh storming her
castle....

Sheikh Kaj al bin Russard—Nothing can keep
him from taking what he wants—and he wants
Catherine. In his life, in his kingdom, in his bed...
but what about in his heart?

King Daniel—The eldest Connelly heir now rules the
picturesque country of Altaria.... But does he control it?

One

"**Y**ou're absolutely right, Kaj," Joffrey Dunstan, Earl of Alston, said in his usual thoughtful way. "She's even lovelier than I remembered."

Glancing away from the slim, auburn-haired young woman who was the subject of his observation, the earl retreated a step from the balcony railing overlooking the grand ballroom of Altaria Palace. Though more than two hundred members of Europe's elite milled down below in their most elegant evening wear, they might not have existed for all the attention he gave them.

Instead, with a bemused expression on his face, he turned to stare at his companion, who stood in a pocket of shadow, hidden from casual observance. "But marriage? You can't be serious."

Sheikh Kaj al bin Russard raised an ink-black eyebrow in question. "And why is that?"

"Because… That is…" Always the diplomat, Joffrey cleared his throat and tried again. "Surely you're aware that Princess Catherine has a certain… reputation. And Sheikh Tarik's will was quite specific—"

"That I marry a virgin of royal blood." Kaj grimaced. "Have a little faith, cousin. I haven't forgotten my father's unfortunate directive. I'd simply remind you that for all Catherine's reputedly wild ways, there's a reason she's known as the ice princess."

"I suppose you have a point. Still…"

Kaj took one last look at the woman he intended to marry, his hooded gray gaze admiring her auburn hair and slim white shoulders before he turned his full attention to his favorite relative.

He was quite aware that, despite the fact their mothers were sisters, there was no physical resemblance between himself and Joffrey. His cousin was five-ten, with a slim build, blue eyes, cropped blond hair and a fair, exceedingly English face. In contrast, he was a trio of inches over six feet, with a distinct copper cast to his skin and ink-black hair long enough to necessitate pulling it back for formal affairs like tonight's.

Yet for all their outward differences, he valued Joffrey's opinion above all others.

It had, after all, been his cousin's matter-of-fact friendship that had eased Kaj's crushing homesickness for his homeland of Walburaq when he'd been sent away at age eight to attend English boarding school. Just as it had been Joffrey's steadying presence and astute counsel that had allowed Kaj to get successfully through Ludgrove and Eton, where he'd stood out like a hawk among pigeons. In all the ways that mattered, Joffrey was the brother Kaj had never had.

The reminder softened the chiseled angles of his face. "If it will ease your mind, Joff, I've made certain inquiries. The princess may be a tease, but she's no trollop. On the contrary. I have it on excellent authority that her virtue is very much intact. Her pleasure seems to come from keeping her admirers at arm's length."

Joffrey's eyes widened in sudden comprehension. "You see her as a challenge!"

Kaj shrugged slightly, his broad shoulders lifting. "If I have to marry, I might at least enjoy the courtship, don't you think?"

"No, I most certainly do not," the other man retorted. "At least not to the exclusion of more important considerations."

Kaj crossed his arms. "And those would be what, exactly?"

"Compatibility. Mutual respect and understanding. Similar values. And...and love." A faint flush of embarrassed color tinted the earl's cheeks at that last, but his gaze was steady as he plowed stubbornly on. "This isn't a prize to be won, Kaj. This is your life, your future. Your happiness."

"Do you think I don't know that?" the sheikh inquired softly. "Trust me. I have no intention of making my parents' mistakes."

Joffrey looked instantly stricken, as well he should since he was one of the few people who understood the price Kaj had paid for Lady Helena Spenser's and Sheikh Tarik al bin Russard's disastrous marriage, bitter divorce and subsequent flurry of heated affairs. "Of course not. I didn't mean to imply you did. It's just that this hardly seems the answer."

"And what is?" Kaj's voice was studiously polite. "Given the need for my bride to be pristine, what are my choices? Should I marry one of those tremulous debutantes your mother keeps throwing into my path? Or should I make an offer for some Walburaqui chieftain's daughter, a sheltered innocent who'll build her whole life around me?" He sighed. "I don't want that, Joff. I want a woman who's pragmatic enough to see a union with me as a mutually beneficial partnership. Not some starry-eyed romantic who'll fall desperately in love with me and expect me to fulfill her every wish and need."

"Ah, yes, adoration can be so trying," Joffrey murmured.

Kaj felt a lick of annoyance, only to have it vanish as his gaze locked with his cousin's and he saw the affection and concern in the other man's eyes. His sense of humor abruptly resurfaced. "More than you'll ever know," he said dryly.

For an instant Joffrey looked surprised, and then his own expression turned wry. "Well, if it's any consolation, I doubt excess worship of you will be a problem with Princess Catherine," he said, matching Kaj's tone.

Kaj cocked his head in feigned interest. "Do tell."

The earl shrugged. "It's simply that the more I think about it, the more I understand your choice. Unlike every other female on the planet, the princess has never shown the slightest tendency to swoon when you walk into the room. And though she may indeed be a virgin—I bow to your superior sources—she doesn't strike me as the kind of woman who'll ever fall at your feet in girlish devotion. As a matter of fact—'' he glanced down at the ballroom spread out below them ''—you'll probably be lucky to get a date.''

Kaj followed his gaze. He quickly noted that Altaria's new king, Daniel Connelly, was about to kick off the dancing with his queen, Erin. Of more immediate interest to him, however, was the discovery that the group of young men vying for Princess Catherine's attention had grown even larger than before. He felt an unexpected pinch of irritation as one would-be swain said something that made her laugh. Vowing to put an end to such familiarity—and soon—he nevertheless refused to rise to his cousin's bait.

Catherine *would* be his. He'd given a great deal of thought to her selection, and one way or another he always got what he wanted. ''I appreciate your concern, Joffrey, but I assure you I'll do just fine.''

''Yes, of course.'' The other man's words were perfectly agreeable, but there was a note of skepticism in his voice that was distinctly annoying. ''I merely hope you're not counting on a quick courtship. Because from the look of things, it may take some time just to breach the crowd around her, much less win her heart.''

''Oh, I think not,'' Kaj said firmly. ''One month should do the trick.''

Joffrey turned to look at him, brows raised. ''You're having me on, right?''

"One month and I'll have Catherine of Altaria in my bed, my ring on her finger. Guaranteed."

Joffrey rocked back on his heels. "*Really.* Doesn't that first part rather violate your father's purity directive?"

Kaj rolled his eyes. "I think not. My intended is supposed to be chaste for me—not *with* me."

"I suppose you have a point."

"I suppose I do."

"In that case... Care to chance a small wager as regards to your success—or lack thereof—in this venture?"

"By all means. Simply name your terms."

"Well, I have always fancied Tezhari..."

Kaj nodded. His cousin had long coveted the exquisite Arabian brood mare. "Very well. As for me, I think the Renoir that graces your drawing room at Alston will make Catherine a lovely wedding present."

Joffrey winced but didn't back down. "It's a deal, then. And may I say good luck. Because in my opinion, you're going to need it."

For the first time all evening, Kaj smiled, regarding the other man with cool confidence. "That's very kind of you, Joff, but unnecessary. This hasn't a thing to do with luck. It's all about skill. Trust me."

At that his cousin laughed. "Why do I suddenly feel as if I should pen the princess a note of condolence?"

The sheikh nonchalantly flicked a nonexistent speck from his impeccably tailored Armani tux. "I can't imagine. But I do hope you'll excuse me." His gaze once more located Catherine down below, and he felt a distinct spark of anticipation. "I suddenly find I'm in the mood to dance."

"Oh, by all means." Joffrey stepped back, clearing the way with a flourish.

A twist of amusement curving his mouth, Kaj strolled away.

"Please, Highness." The handsome young Frenchman at Catherine's side gripped her hand and drew it toward his lips. "You are so very exquisite, with your Titian hair and your *yeux emerauds*. Take pity and say you'll dance with me."

Fighting an urge to roll her "emerald eyes," Catherine told herself to be patient. After all, the ball, for which she'd done the bulk of the planning, was going well. Overhead the thousand tiny lights in the mammoth chandeliers twinkled like iridescent butterflies. The lilting strains of the orchestra were neither too loud nor too soft, and the scent of blooming flowers drifting through the score of French doors thrown open to the mild March night was refreshing rather than overpowering.

Add the men in their sleek black tuxedos, the women draped in silk and satin and a glittering array of jewels, and it was perfect, a storybook scene. Most important to Catherine, the guests of honor—her cousin Daniel and his wife, Erin, Altaria's new king and queen—appeared to be enjoying themselves.

She watched for a moment as they danced, smiling at each other. There was such happiness in the looks they exchanged, such perfect understanding. Out of nowhere she felt an unexpected pang of envy.

What must it be like to share such closeness with

another person? Catherine couldn't imagine. She might be only twenty-four, but she'd long ago concluded that such intimacy wasn't for her.

Her conviction had its roots far in the past, when her nouveau-riche mother had happily surrendered Catherine to the royal family, making it clear in the years since that she regarded her illegitimate daughter as a stepping-stone to high society, nothing more.

It had been further shaped by Catherine's father, Prince Marc, who had always treated her like a unique trinket to be displayed when he wanted, then promptly forgotten once his need to impress others had passed.

Only her grandmother, Queen Lucinda, had ever truly cared for her. But that wonderful lady had passed away five years ago, and her loss had only underscored to Catherine how truly alone she was.

Oh, she had an abundance of suitors, but none of them had ever bothered to get to know the real her, the person beneath the public facade. They were too afraid of making a misstep and losing the chance to win her favor—and with it her money, her connections and, she supposed, her body.

Usually she didn't care. But every once in a while she caught a glimpse of what her life might have been if she'd been born plain Catherine Rosemere, instead of Her Highness Catherine Elizabeth Augusta. And she would suddenly feel unutterably weary of fawning admirers, frivolous soirees and always feeling alone no matter how big the crowd that surrounded her.

Oh, poor, pitiful princess, said a mocking voice in her head. *What a trial to be required to spend time in such a lovely setting, surrounded by the cream of high society. How unfair that you have to wear pretty clothes and listen to a few hours of lovely music and some meaningless chatter. What a tragedy that you're minus your very own Prince Charming.*

One hates to think how you'd stand up to a real problem, like being hungry or homeless. Or wait, how about this—you could be dead, like your father and grandfather, their lives snuffed out in an accident that now appears to have been no accident at all, but rather a deliberate act of murder.

Appalled at the direction her thoughts had taken her, Catherine cut them off. But she was too late to stop the anguish that shuddered through her. Or the guilt that came hard on its heels as she recalled the report by the Connelly family's investigator concluding that the speedboat involved in the disaster had been sabotaged. A speedboat meant to be manned by her, not her father.

"S'il vous plaît, belle princesse." The Frenchman stepped closer, demanding her attention. She looked up to find him gazing limpidly at her, looking for all the world like an oversize, tuxedo-clad flounder. "Do say yes to just one dance. Then I can die a happy man." Practically quivering with anticipation, he pressed his wet mouth to the back of her hand.

The tight rein Catherine had on her emotions snapped. She snatched her hand away, just barely suppressing the urge to scrub it against the delicate chiffon of her midnight-blue dress. "I told you before, Michel, I'm not in the mood. What's more, I'd appreciate it immensely if you'd hold off expiring for at least the next forty-eight hours. Your absence would throw a decided wrench into the seating arrangement for Monday night's banquet.''

The young man blinked. Then, as her words sank in, his smile abruptly vanished. ''But, of course,'' he said, pouting in a way that made him look more fish-like than ever. ''A thousand pardons, Highness.'' Stiff-backed with affront, he turned on his heel and marched off.

Catherine felt a prick of remorse, but quickly dismissed it. After all, she'd been exceedingly polite to Michel the first three times she'd refused his requests to dance. She could hardly be held responsible that he refused to take no for an answer.

Sighing, she glanced at the miniature face of her diamond-encrusted watch. It was barely half past ten, which meant it would be at least another two hours before she could hope to make an unremarked-upon escape. She wondered a little desperately what she could do to make the time go faster.

She was saved from having to come up with an answer as a small murmur ran through the throng surrounding her. A second later everyone in front of her appeared to take a collective step back, clearing a path for the tall, ebony-haired man who strode toward her with a palpable air of leashed power.

Catherine tensed, the way she always did when she encountered Kaj al bin Russard. Although most of the women she knew found the enigmatic Walburaqui chieftain irresistible, she personally didn't care for him. Granted, his chiseled features, heavily lashed gray eyes and beautifully accented English had a certain exotic charm, but there was simply something about him—an innate reserve, the assured, almost arrogant way he carried himself, his indisputable masculinity—that she found off-putting.

She watched as he cut a swath through the crowd like some Regency rake from a bygone age, her edginess increasing as she realized his gaze was locked on her face.

He came to a halt and swept her a slight bow. "Your Highness."

She gathered her composure and inclined her head. "Sheikh."

"I don't believe I've had the chance to tell you in person how sorry I am for your loss."

"Thank you," she replied dutifully. "The flowers you sent were lovely."

He made a dismissive gesture. "It was nothing." He moved a fraction closer, making her intensely aware of how big he was. "Would you care to dance? The orchestra is about to play a waltz. Strauss's Opus No. 354, if I'm not mistaken."

Common sense urged her to simply say no and be done with it. But curiosity, always her curse, got the better of her. "How would you know that?"

"Because I requested it. I believe you once mentioned it was your favorite."

"I see." Ridiculously, she felt a stab of disappointment. In the past two months everything had changed: her father was gone; her position as court hostess was coming to an end; her entire future was uncertain. Now here was Kaj al bin Russard, apparently deciding to join her band of admirers. Though she hadn't liked him before, he'd at least been unique. "How resourceful of you," she said coolly. "Unfortunately, my favorite has changed."

"Then this will give you a chance to tell me what has supplanted it." Without warning he reached out and clasped her right wrist with his long fingers.

His touch gave her a jolt, and for a moment she felt anchored in place by the sheer unexpectedness of it. Then she instinctively tried to pull away, only to find that though he was careful not to hurt her, his grip was as unyielding as a steel manacle.

Her temper flared at the same time her stomach fluttered with unexpected excitement. "Let go of me," she ordered tersely, mindful of the interested stares suddenly directed their way.

"Oh, I think not." Matching her clipped tone, he stepped to her side, planted his hand in the small of her back and propelled her toward the dance floor. "It would be a shame to waste such enchanting music. Plus it just so happens—" he swung her around to face him, waited a beat as the orchestra launched into the waltz, then pulled her close and led off "—I'm curious to see how you'll feel in my arms."

Catherine couldn't believe it. Speechless, she stared up at him. She was shocked at having her wishes ignored, shocked by his statement—and more shocked still by the startling discovery that his hand felt deliciously warm against her cool, bare back.

She shivered as his fingers slid lower, unable to stanch her reaction. Only the sight of the faint smile that tugged at the corners of his mouth saved her from making a complete fool of herself by whimpering or doing something else equally mortifying. "How dare you!" she managed instead, finally finding her voice.

"How dare I not, princess." Never missing a beat, he guided her deeper into the phalanx of whirling dancers. "I could never forgive myself if I let the most beautiful woman in the room remain all alone during her former favorite waltz."

His outrageous flattery, coupled with the realization that he'd noticed her solitary state, brought her chin up. "Is there some reason you're toying with me?" she asked abruptly.

His gaze dropped to her mouth and lingered for an endless second. When he finally raised his eyes, they had a lazy, knowing quality that caused an unexpected clenching in the pit of her stomach. "You really must pay more attention. Toying is hardly my style."

"Just what do you hope to gain from this?" She managed to keep her voice steady, but just barely.

"Surely it's obvious. The pleasure of your company."

"And you believe *this* is the best way to attain it?"

One black eyebrow rose in question. "Isn't it?"

"No," she said flatly. "I don't like being commandeered."

"Ah." His expression lightened. "Does it happen often?"

"Of course not!"

He shrugged, and she felt the steely strength of his body beneath her fingertips. "How unfortunate. Perhaps you simply need to give yourself over to the experience. You might find you enjoy it."

Oh, what nerve! She opened her mouth to reply, then stubbornly shut it again. She would not let him provoke her into causing a scene. She would *not*. Besides, it was time he realized he didn't get to have everything his way. Pursing her lips, she deliberately shifted her gaze to the weave of his impeccably tailored jacket and tried to pretend the rest of him didn't exist.

To her surprise, rather than making another outrageous comment, he actually fell silent. At first she was grateful...until it dawned on her that with the cessation of conversation between them, she was growing increasingly conscious of other things.

Like the hardness of the thigh brushing hers. And the size of the hand now pressed firmly to the base of her spine. Then there was his scent, all dark starry nights and cool desert breezes. Not to mention the warmth that radiated seductively from his powerful body.

Suddenly, she felt...funny. Hot, cold, short of breath and shivery. Alarmed, she tried to pull away, but it was not to be. Instead of letting her go, the sheikh gathered her even closer.

"Princess?"

She felt his heartbeat against her breast, and the funny feeling grew worse. "What?"

"Relax. You're far too lovely to be so unyielding. And far too intelligent not to accept that sometimes the best things in life are those we initially resist."

It was too much. She jerked her head up to stare at him. "I suppose you include yourself in the category of 'best things'?"

He smiled. "Since you see fit to mention it, yes."

"Oh, my. And here I've always believed conceit wasn't a virtue but a vice."

He made a tsking sound. "Such a sharp tongue, little one. But then, the past weeks can't have been easy. Tell me, does it bother you that much to be passed over as Altaria's ruler?''

Well, really! ''Of course not. I've known all my life that women are excluded from inheriting the throne. What's more, Daniel will be an excellent king. He has a very American sense of responsibility and a fresh way of thinking that should be good for the country.''

To her surprise, he actually appeared to consider her words. ''I agree.''

''You do?''

''Yes. I've had occasion to do business with the Connelly Corporation in the past, and found your cousin to be a very resourceful man. Still, it's not Daniel who concerns me, but you. It's never easy to lose a parent. Even a disappointing one.''

Wonderful. And just when she thought he might have some redeeming qualities after all. ''That's hardly any of your business.'' Particularly in light of the second part of the Connelly investigator's report, which had revealed that her father died owing considerable amounts of money due to extensive gambling. The now familiar shame pressed her, but she thrust it away. She had no intention of discussing her father's shortcomings with the sheikh, never mind her failures as a daughter.

He didn't seem to notice the chill in her voice, however. ''My own father passed away some seven months ago. I was never the son he wanted, just as he was never the father I needed. Yet it was still hard to lose him.''

''Oh.'' Suddenly confused, she set her own concerns aside, wondering again if she'd misjudged him—and why he would say something so revealing. "I'm sorry."

"Don't be. Typically, he's managed to complicate my life even now."

"In what way?"

"It seems if I'm to inherit, I must marry."

She was so startled by the disclosure that for a moment she couldn't think what to say. "How...how unpleasant for you."

"Not really. It's been a challenge, but I've finally settled on a wife."

Her budding sympathy evaporated at the complacency in his voice. "I'm certain she's thrilled," she said tartly.

Incredibly, he laughed, a low, husky chuckle that turned several female heads their way and had an odd effect on the strength of her knees. "Perhaps not yet, but she will be." He looked down at her, his eyes gleaming with good humor...and something else.

It took her a moment to identify what she was seeing. And then it hit her.

Possessiveness.

Her breath lodged in her throat as she was struck by a terrible suspicion. In the next instant she found herself reviewing everything that had just passed between them—his sudden attention, his insistence they dance, that surprising revelation about his father. And for the first time she let herself wonder just what was prompting his uncharacteristic behavior. It couldn't possibly be because *she* was the future wife he'd "settled" on. Could it?

Of course not. The very idea was ludicrous. Not only didn't she care for him, she barely knew him, any more than he knew her. And yet, why else would he be looking at her as if she were a prime piece of real estate he'd decided to acquire?

The waltz ended. Determined to make an escape, she looked around, relief flooding her as she spied her cousin, the king, standing alone a few feet away.

"Daniel!" Forcing a smile to her lips, she took a step back the instant Kaj loosened his grip and hastened to her cousin's side, linking her arm with his. "What luck to find you!"

Clearly startled, Daniel tore his attention from his wife, who was threading her way through the crowd, apparently headed for the powder room, and turned to look at her. "Catherine. Is everything all right?" Concern lit his jade-green eyes.

"Yes, yes, of course. It's simply that I was dancing, and then I saw you and realized I'd forgotten to tell you I talked to your mother earlier and she'd like me to visit Chicago soon since Alexandra has asked me to be one of her bridesmaids."

A frown knit her relation's sandy eyebrows. Catherine felt an embarrassed flush rise to her cheeks since she was fairly certain his distress was caused by her rapid-fire statement, rather than the reminder of his sister's recent engagement to Connelly Corporation executive Robert Marsh.

But all he said was, "I see." Before he could comment further, he caught sight of Kaj, his frown disappearing as a welcoming smile lit his face. "Al bin Russard. How nice to see you again."

"Your Majesty."

"I take it you're the one responsible for my cousin's rather breathless state?"

"I believe I am," Kaj said easily.

To Catherine's disbelief, the two exchanged one of those men-of-the-world looks she always found totally irritating. She drew herself up, gathering what was left of her dignity around her like a cloak. "I really do need to talk to you, Daniel."

"Right." With an apologetic smile for the other man, he said, "If you'll excuse us, then?"

Just as Catherine had hoped, Kaj had no choice but to take his leave. With impeccable manners, he tendered the pair of them a bow. "Of course, Your Highness." He shifted his gaze to Catherine. "Princess, thank you for the dance. I look forward to seeing you again."

Not if she could help it, Catherine vowed. With a flick of her head, she turned her back, dismissing him. Sheikh Kaj al bin Russard might not know it yet, but as of this moment she had every intention of excluding him from her life like the unwelcome intruder he was.

Two

"**W**hat are *you* doing here?" Catherine demanded from the doorway of the palace's family dining room.

For all its elegant spaciousness, the room suddenly seemed far smaller than normal, due to the presence of Kaj al bin Russard. The sheikh sat at the far side of the gleaming satinwood table, his suit coat discarded, the sleeves of his white dress shirt folded back, a newspaper in his powerful hands. At the sound of her voice, he looked up. "Princess. How nice to see you."

Catherine stared at him, clenching her teeth against a sudden urge to scream. Taken aback by her reaction, she struggled to rein in her emotions, assuring herself her extreme response to him was merely the result of surprise, frustration and a poor night's sleep. Add to that her worry about her favorite gelding who'd

turned up lame this morning, a meeting with her secretary that had run long so that she needed to hurry
to avoid being late for an engagement in town, and it
was no wonder the unexpected sight of the sheikh
made her feel a little crazy.

"That's a matter of opinion," she retorted, watching warily as he pushed back his chair and rose politely to his feet.

"I suppose it is," he said calmly.

She refused to acknowledge the way her pulse stuttered as he stood gilded by the sunlight that filled the
room or how she once again felt the force of his masculinity. She'd made her decision about him, and the
long hours she'd spent in bed last night tossing and
turning, bedeviled by an unfamiliar restlessness, had
only strengthened her conviction that he was best
avoided.

"I believe I asked you a question," Catherine said.
"What are you doing here?" Last night circumstances had compelled her to be on her best behavior,
but she saw no reason for false pleasantry today.

His gaze swept over her and a faint frown marred
his handsome features. "Are you always this tense?"

Oh! She struggled for self-control. "Sheikh al bin
Russard, this area of the palace is off-limits to every-
one but family. I would suggest that you leave. Now.
Before I'm forced to call security."

A faint, chiding smile curved his sensual mouth but
otherwise he didn't move so much as an inch. "You
really must work on your temper, *chaton.* And not be
so quick to jump to conclusions. As it happens, I had
a meeting with the king this morning. When it concluded, he was kind enough to invite me to lunch.

Regretfully, something came up and he had to leave, but not before he assured me there was no reason for me to rush through my meal.''

An embarrassed flush rose in her cheeks. Stubbornly she ignored it. Daniel wasn't here now and she was. As for the sheikh, he might be fooling everyone else with his designer suits and civilized manner, but she hadn't forgotten the way he'd looked at her last night. Beneath that polished exterior she sensed something intense and formidable, and she wasn't about to lower her guard.

She glanced pointedly at the table, which was bare except for the paper and an empty cup and saucer. ''I see. Well, it appears you've finished, so don't let me keep you.''

''Actually, I was about to have some more coffee.'' He moseyed over to the sideboard and lifted the heavy silver coffeepot off the warming plate, then turned to her, his expression the picture of politeness. ''May I get you a cup?''

For half a second, she considered simply turning on her heel and walking away. Except that she was hungry, since she'd skipped last night's midnight buffet in order to avoid a certain interloper and she'd long since burned off the tea and croissant she'd had in her room at dawn.

She was also certain that if she left now, the sheikh would no doubt conclude it was because of him—and her pride wouldn't allow that. He was already too arrogant by half.

Squaring her shoulders, she strode around the table to the opposite end of the sideboard. ''No. Thank you.''

''As you wish.'' He poured a stream of steaming

brew into his cup and set down the pot. He turned, but instead of returning to the table, he stayed where he was.

She felt his gaze touch her like a warm breeze. And for a moment everything around her—the ivory silk brocade wallpaper, the richly patterned rug beneath her feet, the soothing gurgle of the garden fountain beyond the open windows—seemed to fade as her skin prickled and an unfamiliar warmth blossomed low in her stomach. Appalled, she gave herself a mental shake and tried to convince herself that her response was merely the result of extreme dislike.

It was a delusion that lasted no longer than it took her to snatch up a plate, fill it with cold cuts, fresh fruit and cheese from the buffet, carry her food to the table and set it down.

Because suddenly he was right behind her. "Allow me," he murmured, his bare forearm brushing her shoulder as he reached to pull out her chair before she could seat herself.

The heat from his body penetrated her every nerve ending; she might as well have been naked for all the protection provided by her cream linen slacks and sleeveless yellow silk sweater. Nor could she control the sudden weakness of her knees as his fingers closed around her upper arm and he guided her onto the chair. Or the way the warmth in her middle spread when his palm lingered far longer than was necessary.

Not until he stepped back and released her could she breathe again.

Shaken, she sat motionless on the chair, asking herself what on earth was the matter with her. She'd dealt with a variety of men's advances from the time she'd become a teenager, yet she'd never experienced this sort of acute, paralyzing awareness. It was unnerving.

Worse, it made her feel uncertain and out of control, and that made her angry. "Don't you have an oil deal or a camel auction or something that needs your attention?" she demanded as he picked up his cup, moved around the table and slid into the seat across from her.

"No." He cocked an eyebrow at her and took a sip of his coffee. "All of Walburaq's oil comes from offshore reserves, and its distribution is controlled by the royal family. As for camels, we don't have any since, like Altaria, we're an island nation."

Her annoyance shifted from his presence to his presumption that she was actually that ignorant. "Yes, I know. Just as I know Walburaq is located in the Arabian Sea, was a British protectorate until 1963, declined to join the United Arab Emirates and is currently ruled by your cousin, King Khalid." Doing her best to look bored, she picked up a small, perfect strawberry from the royal hothouse and popped it into her mouth.

"My, my princess, that's very good. I'm gratified that you've taken time to study my country."

She touched her heavy linen napkin to her mouth. "Don't be. It's nothing to do with you." Which was nothing but the truth. Not that she'd ever reveal that her knowledge sprang from a futile attempt when she was younger to impress her father by learning about Altaria's various trading partners. "I've always been good at history."

"Apparently." He took another swallow of coffee.

"It makes me wonder what other hidden talents you possess."

In the process of reaching for another berry, Catherine stilled, her gaze locking with his. She had an uneasy feeling that they'd just moved onto dangerous ground.

It was a sensation that increased as he added softly, "I look forward to finding out."

Alarm shot through her. She parted her lips to tell him in no uncertain terms that wasn't ever going to happen. But before she could say a word, Erin, Altaria's new queen, walked into the room.

Kaj came instantly to his feet. "Your Majesty."

Catherine, schooled in the strict protocol her late grandfather had insisted on, started to rise, too, only to sink back into her chair as her cousin-in-law sent her a remonstrative look. Although Daniel's wife possessed an air of reserve that sometimes made her seem rather distant, one of her first acts upon moving into the palace had been to insist that, among the family, royal etiquette was to be relaxed. It was a necessity, she'd wryly informed Catherine later, since there was little chance that Daniel's very American brothers and sisters would ever consent to bow down and call him Your Majesty.

"Catherine, Sheikh." Erin smiled. "Please, be seated." Letting the footman who'd suddenly appeared pull back her chair, she sat down herself and promptly reached out to touch her hand to Catherine's. "I'm so glad to see you. I haven't had the chance to tell you how much I enjoyed the ball last night. It was simply wonderful. Thank you for showing me how such an affair should be done."

"It was my pleasure," Catherine said sincerely.

The regal young queen gave her arm a squeeze and then turned her attention to Kaj. She sent him a warm and gracious smile. "My husband informs me you've agreed to be our guest."

"I beg your pardon?" Caught by surprise, Catherine couldn't keep the dismay out of her voice.

Kaj shot her a quick glance, and she could have sworn that his hooded gray eyes, so pale in contrast to his inky lashes and olive complexion, held a glint of triumph. Yet as he turned to Erin, his voice was nothing but polite. "It's very kind of you and the king to offer to put me up."

"I assure you, it's no problem. We have more than adequate room."

Catherine had heard quite enough. Setting her napkin next to her plate, she pushed back her chair. "I'm sorry, but I have an appointment in town. If you'll excuse me?" The last was directed toward Erin.

"Why, yes, of course."

She stood, but before she could take so much as a single step, the sheikh was on his feet as well. "Pardon me, ma'am." He bowed to the queen, then immediately turned his attention to Catherine. "Might I beg a favor, princess, and get a ride with you?" His smile—part apology, part entreaty—was charm itself. "I'm afraid I'm without a car today."

Catherine couldn't help herself. "Then how did you get here? Walk?" Erin shot her a startled look and she abruptly realized how she must sound to someone unaware that the sheikh had an agenda all his own. She swallowed. "It's only…I'm running late and I'd hate to cut short your conversation with Her

Majesty. I'm sure one of the servants can drive you later.''

"You mustn't concern yourself with me, Catherine," Erin interjected. "It just so happens I have a meeting in a few minutes."

"Yes, but I really need to go straight to my appointment—"

"I wouldn't dream of inconveniencing you," the sheikh said smoothly. "I'd be honored to accompany you to your appointment. Afterward, if you wouldn't mind, we can go to my hotel and collect my things."

"Good, that's settled, then," Erin said decisively, coming to her feet and heading for the door. "I'll look forward to seeing both of you at dinner."

Catherine simply stood, her face carefully composed so as not to show her horror.

Yet there was no getting around it. Her day had just gone from intense-but-survivable annoyance to major disaster.

Long legs angled sideways, Kaj sat in the passenger seat of the sleek silver Mercedes, watching Catherine put the powerful sports car through its paces.

Pointedly ignoring the ever present security detail following in their wake, she drove as she did everything else. With grace, confidence and—at least where he was concerned—a deliberate air of aloofness. The attitude might have succeeded in putting him off, if not for her breathless reaction to his touch at lunch or the way she'd trembled in his arms when they'd danced last night.

Try as she might to pretend otherwise, she clearly

wasn't indifferent to him. But it was also obvious she had no intention of giving in to her attraction to him.

That alone made her an irresistible challenge, he mused, since he couldn't remember a time when women hadn't thrown themselves at him. And though he'd be the first to concede that some of those women had been drawn by his power and money, he also knew that the majority had been attracted by *him*— his personality, his looks, his unapologetic masculinity.

But not Princess Catherine. To his fascination, she seemed intent on not merely keeping him at arm's length but on driving him away. Not that she had a chance of succeeding...

"Quit staring at me," she said abruptly, slicing into his thoughts.

He settled a little deeper into the dove-gray leather seat. "Now why would I want to do that?"

"Because I don't like it."

"But you're very nice to look at, *chaton.*"

Her grip on the steering wheel tightened. "Do *not* call me kitten," she snapped. "I have a name. And whatever your opinion of my appearance, I dislike being studied like some sort of museum exhibit."

"Very well. If it makes you uncomfortable... Catherine."

Her jaw tightened and he smothered a smile even as he dutifully turned his head and pretended to examine the view.

It was magnificent, he conceded. In between the small groves of palm trees that lined the narrow, serpentine road they were traveling on, aquamarine expanses of the Tyrrhenian Sea could be seen. Red-roofed, Mediterranean-style villas hugged the craggy-

coastline, while a dozen yachts were anchored in the main harbor, looking like elegant white swans amidst the smaller, more colorful Altarian fishing boats.

Yet as attractive as the surroundings were, they didn't interest him the way Catherine did, and it wasn't long before he found himself surreptitiously studying her once again.

He felt a stirring of desire at the contradiction of her, her air of cool containment so at odds with the banked fire of her hair and the baby smoothness of her skin, which practically begged to be touched. She wasn't a classic beauty by any means—her mouth was a little too full, her nose a little too short, and the way her dark-green eyes tilted up at the corners gave her a face a faintly exotic cast. Yet, looking at her pleased him. And made him hunger to do more.

The realization brought a faint frown to his face. Catherine, after all, was going to be his wife. He expected theirs to be a lifelong commitment, and if he'd learned anything from the debacle of his parents' marriage, it was that excessive emotions were not to be trusted. It was all right to find his future bride desirable. Just as long as he didn't want her too much.

Of course, given Catherine's current attitude toward him—and he'd known enemies of the state who'd been treated more warmly—being overcome by uncontrollable lust was probably the least of his worries.

With that in mind, he couldn't resist reaching out and resting his hand on the top of her seat as he turned to face her more fully. ''Where, exactly, are we going?''

For a moment he wasn't sure she would answer.
But then she sliced a quick glance at him. "If you
must know, I like to drop in from time to time on the
various charitable organizations supported by my
family." She took advantage of a straight stretch of
road to accelerate.

"Ah." He pictured her striding down a hospital
corridor, doctors and administrators trailing like so
much confetti in her wake as she looked in on pa-
tients. Or asking pertinent questions of the scientists
at the Rosemere Institute, the cancer research facility
founded by her grandfather.

Pleased by her sense of responsibility, he shifted a
fraction more in her direction, just far enough to slide
his fingers beneath the silken tumble of her hair.

A slight shiver went through her, and her lips tightened. "Today—" without warning she hit the brakes
and made a sharp left turn, dislodging his hand
"—I'm visiting an orphanage."

The explanation was unnecessary since by then
they were sweeping past a high stone wall marked
with a brass plaque that read "Hope House—where
every child is wanted." Beneath that, in letters so
small he almost missed them, were the words,
"Founded 1999 by Her Highness, Princess Catherine
of Altaria." He shot her a startled glance that she
ignored.

Seconds later she slowed the car as they approached a rambling two-story house wrapped by a
wide, covered veranda. Pulling into an adjacent park-
ing area, she switched off the engine, opened her door
and exited the car, all without another word to him.

With a slight shake of his head, Kaj reached for

the door handle. But before he could exit, an explosion of sound had him twisting around. He watched, bemused, as a small army of children burst out of Hope House's front doors, swarmed across the veranda and down the steps, all chattering at once as they ran toward the car.

"Princess, you came!"

"Amalie was ascared you forgot."

"I told her she shouldn't worry. I told her you'd be here soon!"

"Did you bring her a present?"

"Nicco said maybe the new king wouldn't let you visit. He said maybe the new king doesn't like kids like—"

"Children, stop!" To Kaj's surprise, Catherine laughed. It was a husky, musical sound that tickled his nerves like velvet against bare skin. "Of course King Daniel likes you." As she looked down at the dozen small people all vying for her attention, her remoteness melted away. "As a matter of fact, I've told him and Queen Erin all about you, and they've asked if they might come visit you themselves."

"They have?"

"Really?"

"Wait till Nicco hears that."

"Does that mean *you* won't come anymore?" This last was asked by the smallest of the children, a petite black-haired girl with big brown eyes in a too-serious face.

"No, of course not, Amalie," Catherine said gently. "We're friends, no matter what. Yes?"

The child nodded.

"What's more, today is your birthday. I couldn't possibly forget that."

A bashful smile crept across the little girl's face. She sidled closer and leaned against Catherine's hip, rewarded as the princess laid a reassuring hand on her thin shoulder.

Kaj felt a surge of approval. It was good to know the future mother of his children had a maternal side.

Yet even as he told himself he'd made the right choice, that Catherine of Altaria was going to make him a fine wife, he also felt the faintest flicker of uneasiness.

Because just for a second, as he'd watched Catherine's face soften and heard her affection for the children in her voice, he'd experienced an unfamiliar hunger, a desire to have her laugh at something *he* said, a need to have her reach out and touch *him.*

Which was ridiculous, given that he had every confidence that sooner, rather than later, he would be on the receiving end of her affection. All he had to do was stay close and he'd find a way to get past her reserve.

As for this nagging little itch of need she seemed to inspire… It was nothing he couldn't handle.

Three

Catherine sat on the padded chaise longue on her bedroom balcony. She stretched her tired muscles, then huddled a little deeper beneath the ice-green satin comforter she'd dragged from her bed. A golden glow pierced the gunmetal-gray horizon, announcing the sun's imminent arrival and the start of a new day.

For the second night in a row, she'd barely slept. And as much as it rankled to admit it, she knew exactly who was to blame for her second bout of insomnia.

The sheikh. Kaj al bin Russard. Or, as she was beginning to think of him: he-who-refused-to-go-away.

Perhaps she wouldn't be so disturbed if she could write him off as simply another pretty face. Or just a magnificent body. Or even an incredibly willful personality. But the truth was he was all of those things and more.

He was presumptuous, but also perceptive. He was arrogant, yet intuitive. And unlike most of the men she knew, his ego was disgustingly healthy; sarcasm, indifference, even outright hostility all rolled off him like rain off a rock.

Most disturbing of all, his lightest touch was all it took to ignite an unfamiliar fire inside her.

She shivered, not wanting to think about that last bit. Instead she did her best to concentrate on the chorus of birds tuning up to welcome the sunrise—only to make the unfortunate mistake of closing her eyes. The scene at Hope House when Kaj had climbed out of the car yesterday promptly popped into her mind.

Without exception, all the children's eyes had widened at the sight of him. "Who's he?" Christian had asked.

Marko had sucked in a breath. "Is that the king?"

Catherine had been tempted to make a sharp reply—until Kaj had come to stand at her side. The same faint breeze that tugged at his gleaming black hair had carried his clean, masculine scent to her, and suddenly he'd seemed much too close. To her disgust, she'd found she had to swallow hard in order to locate her voice.

"Children, I'd like to introduce Sheikh al bin Russard." Not wanting anyone to get the wrong idea, she'd added, "The sheikh is a friend of my family's."

There were several nods and an "Oh."

And then Christian burst out, "Is he a real sheikh?

Does he live in a tent? How come he doesn't have one of those sheet things on his head?''

Catherine had hesitated a mere instant, and Kaj had stepped into the breach. ''Those sheet things are called ghotras,'' he'd said easily. ''I wear one when I'm in my country, as is the custom. But when I'm here, I try to follow your fashions. And much like you, I live in a home made of mortar and stone. Though I do own several tents. For the times—'' he displayed a quick flash of white teeth ''—when I feel a need to escape and sleep under the stars.''

Whether it was the sentiment or the brief, impish grin that accompanied it, the children all nodded in understanding and several of the boys murmured, ''Yeah!''

Isabelle, one of the older girls, looked earnestly up at him. ''Do you have a camel?''

He shook his head. ''I'm sorry to say, no.'' Although his expression was suitably apologetic, his eyes gleamed with humor as he glanced briefly at Catherine. ''That seems to be a common misconception. What I do have is horses. Beautiful Arabian horses. Oh, and I'm also the keeper of a truly magnificent tiger.''

''You have a tiger?'' Christian, Isabelle and Marko all exclaimed at once. ''A real, live tiger?''

''Mmm-hmm. His name is Sahbak and he was a gift to my father. He's quite a wonderful fellow. Do you know, if you scratch him behind the ears, he purrs?''

''Wow,'' Marko murmured.

That seemed to be the general sentiment. Eyes rounded, the children had stared up at him with a combination of awe and admiration. And though un-impressed by his status as a big-cat owner, Catherine had found that, as the afternoon went along, she couldn't fault his manner. He was wonderful with the children, relaxed, down-to-earth, friendly without seeming too eager. Even little Amalie, who was usually standoffish with strangers, had eventually lowered her guard.

Catherine wanted in the worst way to blame the latter on the exquisite gold coin Kaj had given the child as a birthday present. But honesty forced her to admit it probably had more to do with the coin's presentation. Who would have suspected a Walburaqui chieftain could, with a flick of his long, elegant hands and a widening of his eyes, make a coin vanish once, twice, thrice? Or that, with a subsequent snap of his fingers, he could make it reappear—much to the delight of a giggling little girl—from its hiding place behind one of her shell-like ears?

Certainly not Catherine.

She pulled the comforter up a little higher and sighed. Perhaps it was the earliness of the hour, but for the first time she admitted that keeping the sheikh out of her life was turning out to be more difficult than she'd imagined. And not just because he'd managed to finagle an invitation to stay at the palace, either. But because no matter how hard she pretended otherwise, when she was with him his presence took center stage. A part of her seemed always to be holding its breath, waiting to see what he would do or say next.

Which was annoying but not totally surprising, given the dominant force of his personality.

Far harder to accept was his ability to invade her thoughts. To her horror, every time she let down her guard even the slightest bit he seemed to be there, making her wonder all manner of things.

Like why was he pursuing her when he already had money, power and connections of his own? And what would happen if, in a moment of temporary insanity, she allowed him to get close? How would it feel if she let him kiss her? Or if she let him draw her into the strength of his embrace and touch her? And what would it be like to touch him back, to let her hands roam over his smooth, bronze skin…?

She scrambled off the chaise. Enough, she chastised herself, doing her best to ignore the way her heart was pounding. Clearly two nights of inadequate sleep were addling her brain. A condition that lying around brooding wasn't doing a thing to help.

Her time would be far better spent if she got moving, got some exercise, found a focus for her untrustworthy mind. And the time to start was now.

Impatiently she tossed back the tangled skein of her hair and marched into her room. Fifteen minutes later she was washed and dressed in a white shirt, slim beige twill pants and her favorite knee-high riding boots. She gathered her hair into a high ponytail, snatched up a thin navy vest to guard against the morning chill and slipped out her door.

Kristos, one of her bodyguards, sprang to attention. "Your Highness. Good morning."

She motioned for him to relax. "I'm going for a ride. I promise I'll keep to the palace grounds, so why don't you take a break."

He was clearly not thrilled, but after a moment he

nodded. "I'll let the stable detail know you're on your way."

"If you must." Swallowing a sigh, she started down the corridor, knowing the heightened security was necessary in light of what had happened to her father and grandfather, yet still disliking the increased loss of privacy.

Thanks to the thick, intricately patterned runner that covered the stone floor, the sound of her footsteps was muffled as she began the long, familiar walk toward the west stairway, which was closest to the stables. She reached the intersecting hall that led to the king and queen's apartments, nodded to the pair of guards standing sentinel there, and continued on, moving briskly until she reached a solitary door set midway down the remaining stretch of corridor.

And there she faltered.

She wasn't sure why. After all, she'd passed the entrance to her father's quarters numerous times since his death. And though she'd experienced any number of emotions—disbelief, grief, guilt—not once had she been tempted to step inside.

Until now.

Yet suddenly she wanted to know if Prince Marc had read the note she'd sent him the last day of his life. The note thanking him for going boating in her place with King Thomas and apologizing for disrupting his schedule. The note asking if they might meet later that day so she might explain the real reason she'd begged off at the last minute.

Whether her need sprang from simple curiosity, a belated need to reconnect with her father or some sort of subconscious attempt to occupy her mind with a subject other than the sheikh, she didn't care. She simply had to know. She opened the black-wreathed door and stepped inside.

The elegant sitting room looked the way it always had, as if it was waiting for the prince's imminent return. The carved mahogany furniture was freshly polished, the plush gold, maroon and navy carpet recently vacuumed. Her father's favorite smoking jacket lay folded over the arm of the Queen Anne chair next to the fireplace, and the cut crystal decanter on the wet bar in the corner was three-quarters full.

A lump rose in her throat, but she swallowed it. This was no time for self-indulgence; she'd already given in to enough rampant emotion this morning. Clinging to her composure, she dragged her gaze from her surroundings, crossed the room and let herself into her father's study. She walked to the desk that held his computer and switched the machine on.

Waiting as it hummed to life, she reflected on the contradictions of her father's personality. In so many ways—his belief in the superiority of nobility, his attitude toward women, his resistance to societal change—he'd been a nineteenth-century man. Yet he'd also been fascinated by new technology and had fully embraced the instant access of e-mail. Most likely, Catherine suspected, because without a paper trail he could ignore whomever he chose. In any event, during the past year it had become the best way to communicate with him.

She brought up his on-line server and clicked on the mail-waiting-to-be-read icon. Two entries appeared, and her heart sank as she saw that one of them was indeed hers.

Regret, sadness and a familiar sense of inadequacy washed over her. Well, really. What had she been thinking to harbor even the slightest hope that the prince would have considered anything she had to say of interest? She'd always known she was low on her father's list of priorities.

The only thing that was unexpected was that for once she didn't appear to be alone. Like hers, the other e-mail was timed and dated hours before the prince had left for the marina. Unlike hers, however, the subject line read "urgent."

She frowned, wondering what that could be about even as she clicked the read button and the entire message popped into view.

Your Highness,
The powers that be have agreed to your request, and everything is now in order. As long as the operation continues smoothly, your loan will be reduced as previously discussed.
Your servant,
The Duke

What on earth? Perplexed, she started to read the e-mail again when a faint sound behind her and a sudden prickle at the back of her neck warned she was no longer alone. Unwilling to explain what she was doing—not entirely certain herself—she instinctively clicked off the program before swiveling around.

Gregor Paulus, her father's aide and most trusted servant, stood in the doorway, his usual polite mask firmly in place. "Your Highness. What are you doing in here?"

Although his manner was perfectly civil, there was something in his tone that made Catherine feel like the hapless child she'd been, the one whom Gregor had excelled at discovering at her worst possible moments. Like the time she'd beheaded all her grandfather's prize hothouse orchids to make a bouquet for her nanny. Or the night she'd hidden in her father's closet to surprise him with a good-night kiss only to be trapped when he brought Lady Merton home with him.

She didn't think she'd ever forget the fury in her father's eyes—or the disdain in Gregor's—when the servant had hauled her out of her hiding place the next morning. It most certainly hadn't been one of her more shining hours.

But she wasn't six anymore. She had every right to be here. And even if Gregor didn't agree, it was hardly his place to question her. She drew herself up and stared haughtily at him. "I felt like it. What about you? Isn't it early for you to be on duty?"

He assumed an expression of wounded dignity. "I beg your pardon, but Prince Marc liked having me here first thing in the morning. Carrying on, doing my best to get his affairs in order, is the least I can do to honor his memory." He sounded so sincere that Catherine felt a prick of remorse—until he added piously, "Someone must."

The verbal slap hit its mark. Try as she might to tell herself that Gregor wasn't worth it, that with her father's death he'd lost his power to harm her, his words hurt. Only her pride kept her chin up. The one thing worse than how she felt would be for him to know he'd succeeded in getting to her. "And who better to honor Father than you, Gregor?" To her relief, her voice sounded steady. "No one. So I'll leave you to it."

She could have sworn she saw a flicker of triumph in his pale blue eyes. Yet it vanished as she took a step toward the door and his gaze flicked to the workstation behind her. He stiffened. "Why is the computer on?" he asked sharply.

She shrugged. "I haven't the slightest idea. It was running when I came into the room." She doubted he believed her, but she didn't care. It suddenly felt as if the palace were pressing in on her and all she wanted was to escape. "If you'll excuse me, I'm due elsewhere." She brushed past him, not waiting to hear his response.

Just as she'd intended earlier, she'd go to the stables. By now a groom would have a horse saddled and warmed up for her. Except for the usual exchange with the stable master, she wouldn't have to talk to anyone, much less answer questions or explain herself. She would be able to simply climb into the saddle, take up the reins and head out. She could clear her mind, try one more time to put her feelings about her father into some kind of perspective and drive a stake through any lingering, inappropriate thoughts about the sheikh.

For a little while she'd be free.

Catherine swept into the short end of the L-shaped stable block, her boot heels clattering on the well-swept cobblestones. Blinking as her eyes adjusted from the sunlight to the shadowed corridor, she felt some of the tension drain out of her at the familiar scene.

A dozen roomy box stalls, six to a side, lined each wall, and were occupied by a dozen horses of varying sizes and colors. Some of the animals were still enjoying their morning meals, some were dozing, some stood alertly with their heads thrust out the upper halves of their stall doors. Although there was no sign of another human being, she knew that could be deceiving. "Chalmers?" she called.

There was a sudden movement in the stall to her left and a groom appeared, tipping his head shyly when he saw it was her. "Mr. Chalmers is in the long block, ma'am."

"Thank you, Carlo."

He nodded and she headed briskly down the passageway, swept around the corner—and plowed straight into what felt like a warm steel wall.

Her body knew instantly who it was. Her skin flushed, her nipples puckered, her heart thumped as a pair of strong hands reached out to steady her.

A second later her mind caught up with the rest of her, and she jerked her head up. Just as she feared, she found herself confronted by a pair of bold gray eyes in a familiar face. Her stomach flip-flopped. "You!"

Kaj looked down at her with a wry smile, a faint pair of grooves scoring his lean cheeks. "Good morning, princess."

She parted her lips to ask what he was doing here, then abruptly clamped her mouth shut. She'd asked that question far too often lately, and there was no way she was going to ask it again. Besides, a quick glance at his attire pretty much told the story. Like her he was dressed in a white shirt, breeches and a gleaming pair of tall boots. All he needed to complete his ensemble was a horse.

The discovery was as alarming as his presence. Or would be, she amended, if she gave a whit about how he spent his time. Which she didn't, as long as it wasn't with her.

She pulled free of his hold. "Pardon me," she said sharply, stepping around him. "Chalmers!" She lasered a gaze at the stable master, who stood no more than ten feet away, holding the reins of a compact blood bay as well as a rangy gray. "I assume Cashell is ready?" Not waiting for an affirmative—why else would he be standing there?—she strode forward and snatched the bay's reins from his hands. She glanced at the gray, automatically sliding a reassuring palm down her mount's neck when he pranced sideways. "Why is Keystone saddled?"

Chalmers looked uneasily from her to the sheikh and back again. "Mr. al bin Russard requested him, Your Highness."

Kaj moved to her side. "I thought we might go for a ride."

"Oh, did you?" Once again she moved away from him. Even so, he was still so close that with a sideways glance she could see the faint shadow of beard beneath his bronze skin and a faint scar that bisected his left eyebrow. Out of nowhere, an urge to reach out and touch him—to lay her palm against his cheek, run her fingertips over that inky eyebrow—swept her. Appalled, she wrenched her gaze away and slid the nearest stirrup iron down the saddle leather. "I don't think so."

There was a moment's silence, and then he inquired softly, "Are you all right, Catherine?"

She heard the concern in his voice and looked down to see her hands were shaking. Mortified, she bunched them into fists and rounded on him. "No! Yes! That is, I would be if you'd just leave me alone!"

"Ah." He nodded, his expression almost sympathetic. "I'm sorry, *chaton*, but that's not going to happen."

"Why? Because you have some ludicrous notion that if you hang around long enough I'll marry you?" She regretted the words as soon as she said them. After all, she had no basis for the accusation other than her suspicions. And even if it were true, he'd hardly admit it.

Which was why it was such a shock when he calmly nodded his head and said, "Yes. Precisely."

She stared at him in stupefaction. "You can't be serious! In case it's escaped your notice, this is the new millennium, the twenty-first century! I don't care who you are, you don't get to select a bride the way you would a piece of candy."

"I assure you I put far more thought into this than I would choosing a bonbon," he answered gravely.

"Oh! You're impossible!" She whirled away from him and, before he could make a move to stop her, swung herself lightly into the saddle. Instinctively adjusting her seat as the bay sidled nervously beneath her, she gathered the reins, freed the far stirrup and slid her foot into place. "In the event you still haven't gotten the message, the answer is no. No, I won't go riding with you. No, I won't marry you. Not now. Not ever. For the last time, I want you to leave me alone!'' She urged Cashell forward, not caring as the bay responded with an eager lunge that forced the sheikh to jump out of the way or be run over.

Somehow she found the control to keep the bay at a trot until they were clear of the stable and courtyard. But the minute they reached the path that led to the cliffs above Lucinda Bay, she gave the high-strung gelding his head. With a toss of his silky black mane, the animal leaped into a ground-eating canter that became a flat-out gallop as they turned onto the wide track that skimmed the edge of the headland.

The reckless flight perfectly matched her mood. She'd had enough of reining herself in, of behaving like some witless pushover. She was done allowing Kaj to alternately outrage and sweet-talk her. She was done with him, period. Marriage? What incredible nerve! She didn't even know the man—or him, her.

As for the inexplicable ribbon of loss curling through her, it had nothing to do with the sheikh. Yes, he was charming. Yes, he was attractive, in a purely physical, hormonal sort of way. And yes, she supposed that deep down a tiny, juvenile part of her may have been somewhat flattered by his attention. But that was all it had been; she didn't *care* about him. She didn't.

Cashell stumbled, startling her. He quickly regained his footing, but his misstep was enough to bring her back to the moment. Realizing the bay was tiring, she reined him in, bringing him first to a canter and then to a walk.

That was when she finally heard the sound of hoof-beats, coming on strong. She twisted around in the saddle, incredulous as she saw the sheikh atop Keystone bearing down on her. So what if the Walburaqui chieftain rode divinely, so flawlessly balanced in the saddle that he and the big gray might have been one body? How dare he follow her? How dare he disregard her direct order that he leave her alone?

Catherine couldn't remember the last time she'd completely given in to her temper. But now anger, hot and unfamiliar, bubbled through her. She reined in and waited, and when Kaj caught up with her moments later, bringing the gray to a sliding halt, she let go. "This is the outside of enough, sheikh! I want you to leave this instant—"

He cut her off, saying something in Arabic that sounded as fierce as it did profane. Then he vaulted to the ground, closed the space between them in two big strides, reached up and clamped his hands around her waist.

Catherine stared at him in shock, a funny feeling blossoming in the pit of her stomach. At some point during his ride his rich black hair had come loose and now brushed his open white collar. The bronzed vee of his chest rose and fell with his every agitated breath, while his gray eyes glittered like shards of silver. He looked achingly beautiful, more than a little uncivilized—and every bit as furious as she was.

She told herself that was his problem and vowed not to let him intimidate her, regardless of how formidable he might appear. "How dare you! Let go of me this instant or I swear I'll have you deported!"

"*Bes.*" Enough. He yanked her out of the saddle,

her feet barely touching ground before he gave her a hard shake. "What do you think you're doing, riding so recklessly?" he demanded through his teeth. "You could have broken your neck!"

She blinked. She'd expected him to berate her for her treatment of him, not care about her welfare. Not that it mattered. "Well, I didn't! And even if I had, what I do is none of your business!"

"The devil it's not." He pressed forward, looming over her. "Everything about you concerns me."

"Oh!" She shoved at his broad shoulders, but she might as well have tried to move the promontory they stood on. "Either you're profoundly hard of hearing or simply the most conceited man to ever walk the earth! Whichever it is, I don't give a damn. Just go away!"

"No. And don't swear."

"Or what?" she said scathingly. "You'll say something else I'll choose to ignore?"

She knew she'd made a mistake even before his jaw tightened. Still she wasn't prepared when he abruptly pulled her so close she could feel his heart thudding against her breasts. She parted her lips to protest, but that too proved unwise. With a savage murmur he lowered his head and sealed her mouth with his own.

Her mind reeled. She couldn't believe his sheer audacity. Or that rather than struggling to escape, she was standing statue still, allowing him to take such a liberty. But then, nothing in her life had prepared her for the pleasure suddenly pouring through her in a scalding tide.

The world around her vanished. There was only

Kaj, his heat enveloping her, his scent filling her head, his big, hard angular body the perfect fit for her smaller, softer one.

Far away, she heard someone start to moan. Vaguely she recognized her own voice, but it didn't seem to matter. What was important was the firm, knowledgeable mouth fixed to hers, the tongue breaching her lips, the heat spinning downward to pool in the tips of her breasts and the juncture of her thighs.

She couldn't seem to get enough. Not of the drugging warmth of his kiss, the hands clamped possessively to her hips, the tantalizing friction as their bodies pressed against each other.

He tugged her shirt out of her breeches and slid his hand over her bare abdomen. His thumb swept the lower curve of her breast. She sucked in her breath at the foreign sensation and willed his hand to move higher. When it did, she squeezed her eyes shut, unable to contain a whimper when his fingers closed around her distended nipple.

Her whole body flushed. She arched her back, pressing closer until she felt him, thick and hot against her. Startled and uncertain, damning her lack of experience, she hesitated, not sure what to do next.

Kaj had no such reservation. Reaching down, he slid one powerful arm under the curve of her bottom and lifted her up, bringing her to rest against the bulge of his erection. He pressed her against him, and all the hot, liquid sensation thrumming through her seemed to converge in one aching, sensitive spot.

It was way too much and not nearly enough. Guided purely by instinct, she wrapped her legs around his waist and rocked her hips, rewarded as a groan escaped his lips. He tore his mouth from hers and she started to protest, but the words caught in her throat as he shifted her upper body away from his and his lips found the underside of her jaw. He began to string a chain of kisses downward, into the open vee of her shirt. When he ran out of bare skin, he lifted his head. In the next second his mouth settled greedily over the swollen tip of her cotton-covered breast.

Hot. Wet. Urgent bliss. Sensations flooded her. Who would have thought that being with a man could be like this? That she—justifiably referred to as the ice princess by a legion of spurned suitors—could feel dizzy with desire? Not her.

The idea that she'd finally found a place where she belonged whispered through her mind.

And then it vanished, forgotten as a throbbing, unfamiliar need began to build in her, growing and growing until she couldn't think, couldn't breathe, couldn't stand it a second longer. "Kaj." She pressed her face into the silk of his hair. "Please. Make love to me."

For a moment he didn't seem to hear her. Then he went very still. A violent shudder racked him and the delicious pressure of his mouth at her breast ceased, replaced by the ragged wash of his breath. He slowly raised his head. "Catherine. *Min fadlak fehempt—*"

She might not know the exact meaning of his words but she recognized *no* when she heard it. Even so, for the space of several heartbeats she still didn't understand. And then it struck her. He didn't want her.

An icy fist seemed to close around her heart. As if emerging from a dream, she realized she was clinging to him like a starfish plastered to a rock at high tide. And that despite his obvious arousal, he was still very much in control of himself.

Her desire drained away, replaced by stinging humiliation. For the first time in her life she'd actually wanted a man to make love to her—and he'd said no. Her face burned and it was hard to breathe over the mixture of shame and embarrassment suddenly clogging her throat.

"Catherine?"

She pushed hard against him, and this time he let her go, which she took as a further sign of his rejection. "I...I beg your pardon." Unable to meet his gaze, she addressed the vicinity of his right ear. "This was clearly a mistake."

"No," he said roughly. "You don't understand—"

"Oh, yes, I do." She lifted her chin and forced herself to speak clearly, although she still couldn't bring herself to look directly at him. "I don't know what game you're playing, sheikh, but this never should have happened. Stay away from me. Just... stay away."

To her horror tears suddenly filled her eyes. Not about to break down in front of him, she swiveled on her heel, located Cashell and crossed to him. Her body felt leaden, but somehow she still managed to climb into the saddle where, without so much as a backward glance, she put her heels to the bay's barrel and urged him away.

Back ramrod straight, she pretended not to notice the tears running down her face. After all, there was

no reason for them: it was her pride Kaj had bruised,
not her heart.

She paid no attention to the small, inner voice that
called her a liar.

Four

"Ah, there you are."

At the sound of his cousin's voice, Kaj looked up to see Joffrey step through the wide glass doors that opened onto the palace's west balcony. Backlit by the warm light that spilled from the first-floor drawing room, the Englishman looked dapper as always, his evening clothes impeccably tailored, his pale hair gleaming as he strolled across the exquisitely patterned tiles that comprised the floor.

Reaching a spot just short of where Kaj stood, his back to the balustrade, Joffrey came to a halt. "Getting some air?" he inquired.

Kaj inclined his head. "Yes."

"I must say, it is a lovely night out. Not too warm, not too cold. Full moon, beautiful sky. And while I'm a little disappointed in you, I suppose your aversion to being inside with the rest of us is perfectly understandable under the circumstances.''

''I beg your pardon?''

''I'm referring to Princess Catherine's choice of company this evening, of course. One can hardly blame you for conceding the field. Although personally I've always found that Italian bloke to be a tad cheeky. Then again, if the princess looked at me that way, I'd no doubt feel a bit brazen myself.''

Unable to help himself, Kaj glanced toward the drawing room. Catherine, exquisite in a black lace gown, stood inside next to the grand piano. She was listening intently to something Ricco Andriotti, the internationally known race car driver, was saying to her.

The two had had their heads together all through dinner. By the time the company had quit the table to stretch their legs and mingle, the brash young playboy had even grown bold enough to occasionally touch her. Which he did now, first gesturing ebulliently as he spoke, then reaching out to run a finger down her cheek to underscore his point.

Kaj forced himself to look away, afraid if he watched one second longer he might do something he'd regret. Of course, he wouldn't regret it nearly as much as Andriotti.

''She really does have incredible eyes, doesn't she?'' Joffrey mused. ''And those lashes. They're as thick as the imported paintbrushes Great-Aunt Marietta was so fond of. Add in all that lovely alabaster skin and one can hardly blame Signor Andriotti for wanting to leave his handprints all over—''

''*Shut up, Joff.*''

There was a brief silence. Then Joffrey delicately cleared his throat. "No need to inquire how the court-ship's going, I see. So do be a dear boy and remind me to call home tomorrow. It appears I need to in-struct my people to hurry putting the finishing touches on the stall I'm having readied for Tezhari."

Kaj sliced him a look as sharp as a razor blade. "Tell me, cousin, are you simply feeling reckless to-night, or are you deliberately courting a death wish?"

Joffrey had the brass to chuckle. "Oh, dear. As bad as all that, is it? Would it help if you told me all about it?"

Kaj smiled humorlessly. "I think I'll pass."

"Now, don't be hasty. You know what they say—confession is good for the soul."

"Yes, and silence is golden." Too bad he was the only one who seemed to know it, Kaj thought as he glanced back at the drawing room in time to see Cath-erine smile at something Andriotti was whispering in her ear. To his disgust, the race car driver's hand seemed to have taken up permanent residence on her forearm. He had a brief fantasy of snapping the man's fingers one by one.

Unfortunately, it didn't help that Catherine seemed to be hanging on the Italian's every word. She'd never looked at *him* that way. But then, he might as well be invisible for all the attention she'd paid him to-night. Hell, for the past two days she'd barricaded herself in her room, refusing to take his phone calls or accept either the notes or flowers he'd sent her. And the one and only time their gazes had met this evening she'd looked right through him.

Not that he didn't deserve her scorn. It was bad

enough that he'd lost his temper the last time they'd been together. But to also lose command of the situation, to first lay hands on her and then give in to the temptation to kiss her...

But that wasn't the worst. Oh, no. That designation was solely reserved for how close he'd come to mindlessly stripping Catherine of her breeches and taking her right then and there, out in the open, on the hard ground with nothing but gorse for a bed, where anyone could have seen them.

With no thought for her pleasure, but only his own.

A nerve jumped to life in his jaw. Never, ever, had he experienced such a monumental failure of control, not even when he'd been a raw, inexperienced youth and his father had arranged for a courtesan to instruct him in the art of love.

A part of him still couldn't believe what he'd almost done. And he certainly couldn't excuse it. Any more than he could excuse the clumsy way he'd handled things when he'd belatedly come to his senses. Thanks to his self-absorption, his shock at his behavior, he'd unwittingly hurt Catherine's feelings.

Not that she seemed to be suffering unduly, he noted grimly, his gaze never leaving her.

Nevertheless... For one of the few times in his life, he wasn't sure what to do. He was a man accustomed to taking command; sitting on his hands was no more his style than being on the outside looking in. But what could he possibly say to her? That she made him a little crazy? But not so much that he'd been willing to do what she'd asked and make love to her? He swallowed a sigh. Perhaps, if he gave it enough time, she'd come around all by herself...

"You know," Joffrey said suddenly, "I must say I'm surprised. It's not like you to so readily concede defeat. You still have three weeks remaining, after all."

"I haven't conceded anything."

"Really? You could have fooled me. Hiding out here in the dark, brooding and licking your wounds—"

Kaj frowned, beginning to feel irritated. "I am not brooding."

His cousin regarded him with raised eyebrows. "Then you're doing a bang-up imitation. And may I add, it doesn't suit you."

"What would you have me do? Go in there, grab the princess and cart her off to my room?"

"If that's what it would take to get that pathetic look off your face, yes."

"*Pathetic?*" Kaj repeated in a dangerously low voice. He drew himself up to his full height. "I'm never pathetic—" He broke off as he saw Andriotti sidle even closer to Catherine. Something primitive took hold of him, and his displeasure with his cousin shifted solidly to the Italian.

Joffrey was right, he decided abruptly. Standing around waiting for the perfect moment to approach Catherine wasn't accomplishing anything. It was time to take action. "Excuse me," he ground out, shoving away from the railing and heading for the drawing room.

"Does this mean I should hold off on phoning home?" Joffrey called after him.

Kaj ignored him and stepped inside. Whether it was his grim expression or the purposeful set of his shoulders, the other guests took one look at him and scurried out of his way, clearing a path as he strode toward Catherine.

She and the Italian seemed to be the only two people in the room oblivious to his presence. Though that made him feel grimmer still, he made a conscious effort to unclench his teeth when he reached them. "Catherine. Andriotti." He zeroed in on the smaller man, whom he topped by more than a head, and managed the facsimile of a smile. "Would you be so kind as to excuse us? There's something I need to discuss with the princess."

"Don't be ridiculous," Catherine contradicted immediately, laying a hand on the Italian's arm. "The sheikh is mistaken, Ricco. He and I have nothing to talk about. Nothing at all."

Kaj's gaze flicked from her hand to Andriotti's face. "I would suggest that you go, Ricco. *Now.*"

Whatever the Italian saw in his expression, it was enough to make the other man take a hurried step back. "Yes, of course," he said hastily, sending Catherine an apologetic look. "*Arrivederci, bella principessa. For now.*" With that, he went.

Catherine shifted her attention to Kaj, her exotic green eyes glittering with anger. "You simply don't know when to quit, do you?"

"Let's take a stroll through the gardens," he countered, reaching out to clasp her elbow.

She jerked her arm away. "No. I'm not going anywhere with you." Her voice was frigid enough to cause frostbite.

"Yes," he said, "you are. Your only choice is

whether you prefer to do so under your own power or over my shoulder.''

She stared at him. ''You wouldn't dare.''

He didn't deign to answer but simply raised an eyebrow.

Furious color touched her cheeks. She glared at him for the space of several heartbeats, then with a little ''hmph'' averted her gaze and flounced toward the French doors. He fell in behind her, doing his best not to stare at the lissome line of her exposed back or the enticing sway of her hips.

She crossed the terrace, marched down the wide, shallow steps that led to the gardens, then turned to face him, her slender arms crossed over her breasts. ''Now,'' she said. ''What is it you want?''

Such an interesting choice of words. For an instant he actually considered telling her the truth. *You. I want you. Under me, on top of me, around me. Hot, wet, willing. For however long it takes to sate this exceptionally bothersome hunger you induce in me.*

Yet even without the protectiveness of her posture or the wariness in her eyes, it didn't take a genius to guess how that declaration would be received. Like it or not—and he didn't like it one bit—he was going to have to take a different, far more humbling, tack. ''I'd like to apologize.''

''For what?''

''For what happened between us on the bluff.''

Although he wouldn't have thought it possible, her expression grew even more remote. ''There's absolutely no need for that. You made your regret crystal clear at the time. So now if you'll excuse me—'' She started to step around him, intent on gaining the stairs.

"Catherine, don't." He moved into her path and reached for her.

She jerked back. "Don't you touch me!"

He raised his hands. "Very well. As long as you stand still and listen."

Once again she crossed her arms. "I'll give you exactly one minute. Then I'm calling the palace guard."

He took a calming breath and marshaled his thoughts. "As I said, I'm sorry about what happened. There's no excuse for my behavior, but if you only had more experience—"

"Oh! If you think I'm going to stand here and let you insult me on top of everything else, you're sadly mistaken. Get out of my way. Now!"

"*No*. Not until you hear me out. What I'm trying to say is that you deserve better—"

"Finally something we agree on!"

"—than for the first time we make love to be some quick, mindless encounter. My only defense is that I lost my head. I've known a number of exceptional women, but I've never desired anyone the way I do you. Which, I can assure you, you'd know if you had more experience."

For what felt like an eternity she said nothing. And then he heard her utter a faint, "Oh."

"Make no mistake, Catherine," he said, picking his words with care. "I want you. And I intend to have you. But not until the time is right. Not until you trust me and know that I want you for who you are, not just for the physical pleasure you make me feel."

"But...why bother?" The chilly note had left her

voice, replaced by defensiveness—and a faint note of uncertainty. "Why not just take what you can when it's offered? After all, you've already decided we should marry."

"Because you deserve better. You have a right to expect candlelight and tenderness, to have a man take his time with you. You deserve a lover who makes you feel cherished, not just drunk with desire. You shouldn't have to settle for a quick toss in the grass with someone you don't trust."

Again she was silent. Then, after what felt like a very long time, a sigh escaped her lips. "I don't understand you, Kaj," she said softly. "I don't understand you at all."

"All I want is a chance, *chaton*. A chance for us to get to know each other, to spend some time together. Perhaps we'll find we don't suit. But then again, perhaps we'll find we do. What can it hurt to find out?"

The question seemed to hang in the moonlit air between them. "I'm not sure," Catherine answered finally. "But you may not feel that way when you learn that I decided a long time ago that I'd never marry. You or anyone else."

"So perhaps I'll have to settle for our being friends."

"Do you mean that?"

"I always mean what I say." It wasn't a lie. He did want to be her friend, just as he wanted to be her lover. That he still intended to marry her despite her naive and unrealistic, if rather touching, intention to remain unwed, was a mere detail. One he had every confidence she'd come to view the way he did, as a practical necessity, once they spent more time together.

After all, she had no place here in Altaria now that Prince Marc was dead, while as the wife of Sheikh al bin Russard she'd have a position in society, unlimited wealth and the personal freedom to do whatever she liked. She was an intelligent woman; given a little time and the proper attention, she was certain to see the advantages of a union between them.

"All right," she said a trifle breathlessly. "As long as you understand how I feel."

"I believe I do. Now, what do you say to the proposition that we get away from the palace tomorrow?"

"To do what?"

He smiled. "I can't tell you that, Catherine. It would ruin the surprise. Simply say you'll meet me at the south portico at noon." By then he'd have figured it out himself, he thought wryly.

"All right. I'll be there."

"Good. Then there's just one more thing." Eliminating the space between them, he cupped her face in his hand. Her cheek felt baby smooth against his fingers, her jawbone light and delicate.

Apprehension flared in her eyes. "Kaj... I don't think—"

"Hush." He pressed his thumb to her lips; he knew he was taking a chance, but the need to erase every trace of Andriotti's touch on her was riding him hard. "Trust me." He slid his thumb to the base of her chin and lowered his head, ignoring the heady rush of need that deluged him as he settled his lips against hers.

Damn, she was sweet. Her scent, her taste, the texture of her skin...all of it pleased him. For a few seconds he let his hunger off its leash, sliding his arm around her, finding the bare valley of her spine with his hand, allowing himself the sheer sensual luxury of exploring that warm satin hollow with his fingertips.

Yet he had no intention of jeopardizing their newfound understanding. Just as quickly as he'd let himself go, he reined himself in, shifting his hand to the lace-covered indentation of her waist and easing his mouth away from hers.

"Ah, you're such a temptation," he murmured, pressing a kiss first to one corner of her lips, then her cheek and finally her temple. He rested his forehead against hers, allowed himself a moment to catch his breath, then eased back. He looked down at her with a rueful smile. "But I swear to you that the next time we kiss—if there is a next time—it will be only at your invitation. Now, we'd best go in, before you succeed in unmanning me completely."

Even in the moonlight he could see the look of satisfaction that crossed her face, and he congratulated himself. Admitting to a temporary weakness couldn't be all bad if it succeeded in restoring her self-esteem.

"Come." He held out his hand and after the briefest hesitation, she took it. Try as he might, he couldn't entirely contain a sense of triumph. Or quiet the deadly serious little voice that whispered, "Mine," as, side by side, they headed inside.

Five

"**A**mazing," Catherine murmured, still trying to take in the sight before her: the glistening blue-white ice filling the temporary skating arena, the bubble dome enclosing it, the stereo speakers issuing pop music.

It would have been a surprise even without the presence of the children from the orphanage. But they were very much in attendance, dotting the ice like sprinkles atop an ice-cream cone. Some clung to the tubular rail that encircled the rink, some stood windmilling their arms in desperate bids for balance, some were actually gliding around the mirrorlike surface. All together they were as noisy as a convocation of crows, expressing their delight in their surroundings with a mixture of shrieks and laughter.

Catherine turned to look at Kaj, unable to keep the

wonder out of her voice. "Whatever made you think of this?"

He shrugged. "Your cousin Daniel deserves some credit. He and I were enjoying a game of chess the other night when he mentioned you'd visited his family one winter in Chicago, learned to skate and had seemed quite taken with it."

"But that was a decade ago, at least. I can't believe—" She broke off as she realized she was about to say, You went to so much trouble to please me. Taken aback, since she certainly didn't consider herself as needy as such a declaration implied, she deliberately lightened her voice. "That is, however did you manage this? Skating rinks don't grow on trees, and there's certainly never been one in Altaria."

"I have an acquaintance in the amusement business in Trieste. I made a phone call. He took care of the rest."

He was obviously downplaying his role. Even if his friend had all the equipment to put together an ice arena in less than twenty-four hours, Kaj still would've had to secure the site, get a permit, arrange for power and water hookups and take care of a dozen other things she was no doubt overlooking.

"The most challenging part was having it ready by this afternoon," he confided. "It seems this much water takes a certain amount of time to freeze."

"Surely you realize I could have waited a day."

He shook his head. "I promised you a surprise. As I believe I've mentioned before, I always mean what I say."

To her dismay, his declaration made her suddenly remember something he'd said last night. *Make no mistake, Catherine. I want you. And I intend to have you.*

And just like that her mouth went dry and her nipples tightened. Hastily she crossed her arms, reminding herself sharply that that had been before. Before she'd made it clear that marriage wasn't for her. Before he'd conceded the most they might ever be was friends. Before he'd demonstrated his good faith by bestowing a kiss on her that had been a model of respect and restraint.

As for the tiny but willful part of her that persisted in hungering for more—it was her cross to bear. While Kaj's explanation for putting a halt to their encounter out on the bluff had eased the worst of her hurt and embarrassment, it wasn't an experience she had any intention of repeating. And surely, given time and familiarity, the shivery feeling she got when she was around him, as well as the zing of pleasure she experienced at even his most innocent touch, would dim. It had to, since the alternative was simply unthinkable.

"What about the children?" she asked. "What made you think to invite them?"

"Self-preservation." At her startled look, the skin around his eyes crinkled. "Given recent events, and your effect on me, princess, I thought it would be best for us to be chaperoned."

Some of her anxiety eased. "I'm glad you did. Otherwise, I suppose I'd have to skate alone, since I don't imagine they do much ice-skating in Walburaq."

"You forget I went to school in England."

"You skate?" She tried to picture it and couldn't.

He was simply too big, too intent, too seriously masculine for something so lighthearted.

A rueful smile curved his mouth. "In a manner of speaking. My mother's family has an extensive holding in Northumberland, and my cousin Joffrey and I spent our winter holidays there. He made certain I learned the local pastime. Initially, I've no doubt, because he enjoyed seeing me fall."

She considered his wry expression. "You're not serious."

"Ah, but I am."

"But I've met your cousin. Blond, rather serious, lovely manners?" He nodded his confirmation, and she couldn't contain a protest. "He seemed so civilized."

"A facade, I assure you," he responded dryly. "A devil in tweed would more accurately describe him."

As if a veil had been torn away, she suddenly heard the affection underlying his tone. "The two of you are close?" As fond as she was of her own cousins, she'd never spent much time with them. The idea that Kaj had a warm relationship with a member of his family, particularly one who seemed so different from him, was oddly endearing.

"Very. Despite his limitations as a skating teacher. Not to worry, however. Today I thought I'd limit myself to just being an observer."

She forgot all about their respective families. "No. You can't!"

One elegant black eyebrow rose. "I can't?"

"No." The mere idea of being watched by him made her skin tingle; she didn't want to think how her body would react to the real thing. "You can't go to all this trouble and then just sit on the sidelines like some kind of all-powerful pasha expecting to be entertained.''

"But I *am* a pasha, dearest Catherine, albeit an Arabian one.''

"Not today,'' she said firmly. "Today you're a participant.''

Their gazes met. He studied her a moment, and then his face softened and he inclined his head. "Very well. If that's what you wish.''

Her stomach did an unexpected flip-flop, and once more she tried to tell herself the cause was nothing more than sexual chemistry. Only, this time she didn't totally believe it.

She liked him. Or at least she could, she quickly amended, if this was the real him and not some carefully constructed act. Which she didn't think it was.

Not that *that* was necessarily good. She could handle being physically attracted to him, though it wouldn't be easy. But to actually become friends, to have someone in her life who was genuinely interested in her, who wanted to know her in more than just the Biblical sense...

She drew in a shaky breath. Giving him a second chance had seemed like the right thing to do last night. But now she wasn't so sure. Could she trust her instincts? Could she trust *him?* Or *was* she really so needy, so starved for attention, she'd lost all perspective? Even worse, what if she was just looking for an excuse to go after what she'd already decided she shouldn't have?

"Catherine.''

She jumped as he touched his palm to the small of her back. "What?"

"Quit thinking so hard." He urged her toward a bench near the curving, puffy plastic wall. "Today is about having fun. Relax." He motioned to a young man standing next to a large chest.

"I am relaxed." It wasn't a total lie, not really. As soon as she put some space between them—and got away from the delicious weight of his hand resting against her—she hadn't a doubt she'd feel much, much calmer.

She took a jerky step and abruptly sat down on the end of the bench, feigning interest in the youth approaching with a pair of large, square boxes. He set them down, retrieved two pairs of skates, and in no time at all she and Kaj were booted and laced.

"You're certain I have to do this?" Underlying Kaj's inquiry as they headed for the ice was a distinct note of reluctance.

"Yes."

He uttered a faint sigh, and to her surprise, she found she wanted to smile. Although it was hardly to her credit, there was a part of her that was looking forward to seeing him be less than his usually competent self.

But first she had a more immediate concern. The instant she stepped onto the ice, children approached from every direction, drawn to her like filings to a magnet. "We've been waiting and waiting for you," Marko exclaimed.

"Watch me, Princess Cat!" Christian demanded, doing an awkward pirouette.

"Look at my skates!" Isabelle pointed at her feet. "Aren't they pretty?"

"Will you skate with me?" Elizabeth asked.

"Me, too?" Nicco chimed in.

Just for a moment Catherine wondered what it would feel like to be free of obligation. The thought quickly faded, however, as she looked around at the faces turned hopefully up at her. If there was one thing she understood, it was a child's need for adult recognition. She summoned a smile. "Of course I will—"

"But later," Kaj said firmly. "First Her Highness needs to practice." He ignored the chorus of dejected oh's that greeted this pronouncement and leaned close to Catherine, his warm breath tickling her ear. "Quit looking so surprised. You deserve some time just for you." Straightening, he addressed the children. "I, however, would be delighted to skate with you. Or perhaps some of you might prefer to have a ride on my shoulders?"

There was an instant uproar. "I want a turn!"

"Me first, me first!"

"No, me!"

He raised a hand to silence the jangle of young voices, looking around until his gaze settled on Amalie, who was hanging back as usual. "What about you, little one? Would you like to go skating with me?"

She considered, then shyly nodded.

"Very well." As easily as that, he leaned down, turned her around and gently lifted her up, settling her squarely on his broad shoulders. "Don't worry," he murmured as the child took a death grip on his hair. "I won't drop you."

"Promise?" came her tremulous voice.

"On my honor."

Amalie thought about it, then relaxed enough to give him a tentative pat on the head. "'Kay."

He took in the other children's disappointed expressions. "Everyone who wants one will get a turn," he said, and the youngsters' faces immediately brightened. He turned to Catherine. "If you'll excuse us?"

Hopelessly if reluctantly charmed, she nodded. "Of course."

He nodded back, then turned and skated away, skimming over the ice so effortlessly he might have been born with blades on his feet.

So much for incompetence! She'd been conned, and though she told herself she ought to be mad, it was impossible. Still, she couldn't allow him to escape completely unscathed. "Has anyone ever told you you're a scoundrel, Sheikh al bin Russard?" she called after him.

He executed a graceful half turn so he was gliding backward. His teeth flashed whitely. "As a matter of fact, yes. I believe they have."

Oh! The man had more nerve than anyone she'd ever known. Which was precisely what made him so entertaining.

Deliberately she turned her back on him, doing her best to ignore the amusement dancing through her like sunlight on water. Still, she couldn't seem to stop smiling even as she took a few tentative steps of her own. To her delight, so quickly did she find her footing, it might have been days instead of years since her last outing. In no time at all she was lost in the sheer exhilaration of flying over the ice, and the next hour flew by. By the time she finally conceded to a break to catch her breath, she felt as giddy as a teenager.

And every bit as mischievous. Gliding out of the far corner, she eyed Kaj, who stood down the rail, standing to one side of a half circle of attentive children. Carefully judging velocity and distance, she sped up, then slid to a showy stop—a move that just happened to spray a certain Walburaqui chieftain with a shower of ice.

The children gasped. Then the gasps turned to smothered giggles at the sight of the frosty coating clinging to the sheikh's face. "Uh-oh," Marko murmured as said sheikh turned to consider Catherine.

Kaj deliberately wiped the clinging crystalline droplets from his face before raising one black eyebrow. "Having fun?"

She smiled sweetly at him. "Yes. I am. Thank you for asking. And you?"

His gaze flicked to her upturned mouth. Just for an instant something hot and dangerous seemed to flare in his eyes. Then he smiled and his whole face changed, leaving her to wonder if she'd just imagined that torrid look. "Yes, I believe I am. Despite a certain person's warped sense of humor."

"We're all having fun," Christian chimed in brightly. "But it would be even better if you'd skate with us, Princess Cat."

Wrenching her gaze away from the sheikh, she glanced around to find the children all staring expectantly at her. Grateful for the distraction, she nodded. "I'd be delighted."

"Good!"

"I want to be first," Isabelle declared.

"No, me!" Marko chimed in.

Christian pursed his lips. "How about if we all hold hands? Then everyone can skate together!"

- There was a moment's silence as his suggestion was considered, then a sea of small heads bobbed up and down.

"Is that all right with you, Mr. Kaj?" Elizabeth asked, staring up at him with a worshipful expression.

"Certainly." He glanced at Catherine. "What do you say? Want to give it a try?" He held out his hand.

Once again she looked into his handsome face, her heart giving a familiar little stutter as their fingers brushed. "Yes," she said impulsively, "that would be—"

"Perfect!" Christian thrust between them, bristling with importance. "You can be on the inside, sheikh, because you're the biggest. And Princess Cat can be at the other end—" he took Catherine's hand and tugged her toward the rail "—because she's the fastest. And everybody else can be in between." He gestured at the other children to fall in.

Catherine glanced over her shoulder at Kaj, expecting him to protest. When instead he gave a philosophical shrug, she felt a prickle of disappointment.

She looked away, telling herself not to be foolish. The last thing she needed was to hold hands with the sheikh like some sort of vapid schoolgirl. Yet she couldn't deny the pang she felt when she glanced back and was just in time to see him reach down to clasp little Isabelle's skinny fingers with his much bigger ones.

In that instant she knew she'd been deluding herself.

Despite all her protestations to the contrary, what she wanted from Kaj al bin Russard was not a platonic friendship. So what, exactly, did she want?

Kaj strode along the headland path, moonlight lighting his way. Like a lover's playful fingers, the ocean breeze skimmed over his face, plucked at his white silk shirt, tugged at his pulled-back hair. He barely noticed. He was far too intent on identifying the cause of the uncharacteristic restlessness powering his steps.

He tried to tell himself it was merely the result of his longing for home. As had often happened during his school years in England, he was fed up with well-ordered gardens, constricting clothes, too many people and too many rules.

He wanted—no, he needed—to strike out with a few trusted kinsmen, to lose himself in the vast silence of the desert where he could travel for days seeing nothing more than a sun-drenched horizon or the endless black dome of a star-spangled sky. He needed to shake off civilization, speak his native tongue, drink in the hot, dry desert air and not this softly misted imitation fluttering in off the Tyrrhenian.

And it certainly wouldn't hurt if somewhere in there he could take Catherine to bed.

The last thought brought a sudden, reluctant smile to the tense line of his lips.

Very well. So perhaps there was more to his present mood than mere homesickness. Something resembling an ocean-size pool of lust that rose with each passing day, threatening to breach the dam of his restraint.

Ah. And I suppose that explains why finding a way to coax a smile from Catherine has become such a priority. Or why she's constantly on your mind. Yes, and let's not forget the growing need you have to protect her from any and every hurt.

He stubbornly gave a mental shrug. The truth of the matter was he'd always had a penchant for defending those weaker or less fortunate than himself. How could he not? Both his parents had been so self-absorbed while he'd been growing up that someone had had to look out for the hundreds of people who looked to the Russards for guidance, protection, support. He'd had no choice but to step in and do what had to be done.

As for Catherine, she understood duty and obligation, was exceedingly nice to look at, had breeding as well as style—just as he'd foreseen when he'd chosen her to be his wife. Of course he wanted to protect her. She now belonged to him, whether she wanted to or not.

That he found her interesting was simply an added bonus. As was her underlying kindness and the vulnerability she did her best to hide with her tart tongue and that raised, elegant chin. He was beginning to understand her well enough to know she'd deny she needed, much less wanted, a champion. But he hadn't missed her extreme surprise and genuine delight today at the skating rink—and he was glad for the

chance to make her happy. If nothing else, having her
depend on him could only benefit the long-term success of their marriage.

*Yes, of course. But how does that square with your
growing possessiveness?*

Kaj hunched his shoulders and lengthened his
stride. There was no way he could outpace his own
misgivings, however, and after a moment he had to
concede that that development was a trifle unsettling.
Although he'd always viewed women as fascinating
and complex, he'd also seen them as fairly inter-
changeable. If an association with one didn't work
out, there was always another charming creature waiting to step into the breach.

Yet for some reason he didn't feel nearly so cav-
alier about Catherine. She was *his,* and while it made
perfect sense that the idea of her being with anyone
else was absolutely unacceptable, at some point during their little skating party today he'd realized she
was the only woman he wanted. At least for the present—and even that was unprecedented.

Not to mention crazy. If he didn't get a firm hold
on such fanciful thinking and soon, the next thing he
knew he'd be wondering if perhaps he was on the
verge of falling in love.

He abruptly stopped walking, which was just as
well, since he'd reached the farthest point of the
promontory. Thrusting his hands in his pockets, he
blanked his mind, disgusted that he would entertain
such a ridiculous idea even in passing.

With an iron will he forced himself to concentrate
on the waves down below, watching as they dashed

themselves against the projecting jumble of rocks, retreated, then came rushing in again.

He wasn't sure how much time passed before he realized he found the age-old action decidedly suggestive.

The discovery startled a laugh out of him, and like a puzzle piece snapping into place, he suddenly realized he'd been correct at the start of his walk. His uncharacteristic mood really *was* just frustrated desire. Catherine was the first woman to hold herself aloof from him, and as Joffrey would put it, he was in a "bad way." The fact that such a thing had never happened to him before explained why he'd allowed himself to get caught up in all these other unacceptable thoughts and uncertainties.

But now he knew. He wanted Catherine, pure and simple—and not just to fulfill the dictates of his father's will. Oh, no. He was way past the point of making her his solely out of duty. When he finally claimed her, he wanted her hot, slick, wet, whimpering with need, straining against him, her legs locked around his back, begging him to sheath every thick, aching inch of himself in the tight glove of her womanhood.

Even as his body throbbed at the images tumbling through his mind, he breathed a sigh of relief. Looking back on the day from this new perspective, he thought it safe to say he'd made definite strides toward achieving his goal. The skating idea had been nothing short of inspired, and Catherine had clearly been pleased. Add in his gentlemanly behavior, and he'd made definite progress in winning her over.

The next step would be more of the same. After

that, he'd find a way to get her off by herself, away from the palace, away from her friendly group of orphans, away from all other distractions.

Once he got her truly alone, she'd have no choice but to focus solely on him. And once she did, it shouldn't take much to get her into his bed. Then finally all these disturbing and uncharacteristic doubts would be vanquished for good.

As for the fantastical notion that he could be falling in love—it was absurd. Truly, absolutely, unequivocally absurd. Hadn't he seen what "love" had done to his parents and everyone around them? Hadn't he vowed never to get caught in a similar trap?

Absolutely. And he had no intention of changing his mind, now or ever.

No matter the temptation.

Six

"**Y**ou, my dear *chaton*," Kaj said, "are a menace."

Accepting his steadying hand as she climbed out of the gleaming-hulled cigar boat, Catherine turned to look up at him the instant her feet touched the palace dock. "I beg your pardon?"

"You heard me." He jumped lightly down beside her. Wrapping his long fingers around her upper arm, he gently urged her toward shore as the dock attendants moved in to secure the mooring ropes. "Was there some purpose in cutting in front of that ocean liner? Other than giving me a heart attack? Or attempting to make my hair turn white?"

She glanced at the hair in question. Black as a winter night, as shiny as a raven's wing, several of the thick, straight strands had come loose from the leather thong anchoring them at his nape and now framed the strong angles of his sun-kissed face. Her fingers suddenly itched to touch him.

She looked away, filled with the by-now-familiar confusion she'd been immersed in since they'd gone skating.

The past handful of days had been amazing. She and Kaj had spent most of their waking hours together, engaged in activities from horseback riding to dancing the tango at Altaria's hottest nightclub. They'd gone on a picnic, spent an afternoon hang gliding, flown to Rome for a day of shopping, stayed up an entire night playing a cutthroat game of baccarat, which Kaj had waited until after he'd won to cheerfully inform her was Walburaq's most popular pastime.

Such were his persuasive abilities, he'd even convinced her to show him Altaria from the water—no mean feat since she hadn't gone near a boat since losing her grandfather and father.

Most amazing to Catherine, through all the things that they'd done, was how they'd talked. Perhaps not about their most private feelings—she still couldn't bear to discuss her father or the circumstances surrounding his death—but about more than fashion or the weather. To her surprise she'd shared happy memories of her grandmother, admitted how as a child she'd longed to go to a real school rather than be tutored, had even talked about her Connelly cousins and how she'd always envied them their bonds with each other.

For his part, Kaj had regaled her with tales of his schooldays in England, disclosed some of the difficulties he'd had growing up caught between two cultures, revealed an unexpectedly sentimental side when he'd described the ancient fortress built around an oasis that was his home.

And though none of their conversations had seemed particularly serious at the time, at some point Catherine had realized she knew that Kaj's parents' marriage had been an unhappy one, that he had no intention of repeating that particular bit of family history, and that for all his easygoing charm, he took his responsibilities seriously.

She'd also learned firsthand that he really was a man of his word. Just as promised, except for legitimate reasons like holding her when they danced, shielding her from the occasional paparazzi or helping her in and out of various vehicles, he'd kept his hands to himself. He'd been gallant and gracious, thoughtful and polite, concerned at all times with her comfort and pleasure—the perfect gentleman.

And it was starting to make her a little crazy. When they were apart, she wondered where he was, what he was doing and with whom. When she was with him, she wondered what he was thinking. And all the while her senses seemed to be operating on overdrive. A part of her was constantly tracking everything about him—the tone of his voice, the warmth that emanated from his skin, his scent, his relative proximity, his facial expression.

She was starting not to recognize herself. She'd tried to convince herself that her unusual behavior was the result of prolonged sleep deprivation, since she hadn't slept through an entire night since their first meeting at the ball—but she didn't really believe it. Something else was happening, and she was very much afraid she knew what it was.

He was getting under her skin, sweeping her off her feet, making a place for himself in her heart.

She had no intention of letting him know that, though. What she felt was too new, too unexpected, too fragile and ultimately uncertain to share. She was having a hard enough time explaining it to herself.

Suddenly aware that he was still waiting for a response to his accusation that she'd tried to scare him, she did her best to match his light manner. "Don't be such a baby. Everyone knows that big ships are notoriously slow. Plus we had scads of clearance time, and I was only at three-quarters throttle. Although I have to admit, I did love hearing the warning horn blare out. It sounded wonderfully dramatic, don't you think?"

His response would have been deemed a snort had it been made by anyone half so sophisticated.

She felt the corners of her mouth start to curve up, but quickly controlled herself. "In any event," she said, trying to sound austere, "I'd watch whom I criticize, sheikh. Let's not forget just who it was who attempted to take that wave sideways and very nearly flipped the boat. In the future you might want to consider sticking to those things you know."

"Very well. If you insist." He ceased his unhurried walk and pulled her around to face him. Then, his movements deliberate, he moved his hand slowly up her arm, slid it under her hair and cupped the back of her neck. "I'm just not sure where around here—" he lowered his head so she felt his warm breath against her lips, and her eyelids suddenly felt heavy "—I'd be likely to find a camel. Do you?"

It took a second for his words to sink in. When they did, her lashes snapped up and she found he was mere inches away.

He raised an eyebrow at the same time that a slow, devilish smile transformed the perfection of his lips. "What? You were expecting me to ravish you?"

She laughed. The sound burbled softly up, the result of an odd combination of exhilaration and embarrassment. "The thought did cross my mind," she admitted recklessly.

He shook his head and a loose strand of his hair tickled her cheek. "Not until I receive an invitation."

"Yes. So I understand." And finally she did. With a sense of wonder, she realized she trusted him. Enough to take a chance.

Her gaze locked with his, she brought her hand up and brushed his hair behind his ear. The errant lock was silkier than she'd expected, as was the arch of his ear. Intrigued, she traced the curve of his jaw with her fingertips. His bones felt larger, denser than her own, but his skin was surprisingly smooth despite the faint prickle of beard that lurked just beneath the surface.

"Catherine—"

"Shh." Then she breathed in, filling her head with the essence of him, a heady combination of spicy aftershave, soap, saltwater and sun, and suddenly such limited contact wasn't nearly enough. Sliding her hands around his neck, she pushed his collar out of her way, took a half step forward and buried her face in the warm hollow where his neck met his shoulder.

As it had that day on the cliffs, pleasure enveloped her. Only this time there was none of the frantic urgency, the uncertainty of being completely out of control, to distract from the experience of being close.

She closed her eyes, soaking up sensations like a sponge. She felt the steady thud of his heart against his chest, the hardness of his thighs through the finely spun material of his slacks. His chest was broad, solid, warm, a welcome refuge protecting her from the breeze blowing in off the water.

It was the smooth, taut, velvety texture of his skin beneath her cheek that made her head spin, however. With a sigh of pleasure, she snuggled closer, more than a little intoxicated by the pleasure of being in his arms.

She wasn't sure how long they stood there, bodies pressed together. Finally Kaj made a sound that was midway between a chuckle and a groan. "I was right," he murmured, his lips brushing her temple. "You *are* a menace." The words might have stung if hadn't added, "A beautiful, much too desirable one." His movements firm but gentle, he reached up, disengaged her arms from around his neck and set her away from him. "Now come." Linking his fingers with hers, he resumed his unhurried walk. "Let's see if we can't find some refreshment. I find I'm feeling a little overheated."

Any embarrassment she might have felt was banished by his admission. "I believe I could use something cold to drink myself," she conceded, breathless but happy as she strolled beside him. "And something to eat. All of a sudden I'm famished."

In companionable silence they reached the end of

the dock, crossed a swath of emerald lawn edged with bright splashes of blooming flowers, and proceeded up the wide stone staircase that led to the palace's main back terrace.

They hadn't taken more than a step or two across the tile floor of the gallery when a movement in the shadows of an archway to her right caught Catherine's eye. Her attention arrested, she came to a halt, tensing as Gregor Paulus emerged from the darkness.

He inclined his head. "Your Highness. Sheikh al bin Russard."

Something in the way his gaze flicked from her to Kaj and back again made her suspect he'd been watching them for some time, an idea she found extremely distasteful. "What is it, Gregor?" she demanded.

"Might I have a moment of your time?"

"Is it really necessary?"

"Yes, Your Highness. As much as it pains me to interrupt your…tête-à-tête, I believe it is."

She bit back a sharp reply. Sinking to his level would accomplish nothing. "Very well." She glanced at Kaj. "Would you excuse me? This shouldn't take more than a second."

Flicking a speculative look at the servant, he nodded. "Of course. I'll wait here for you."

She smiled, then turned away. As she approached Gregor, he stepped back into the gloom of the shadowed archway, beckoning her to follow with a crook of his long skinny fingers.

She barely had time for her eyes to adjust to the change in light when he came straight to the point. "I found this among His Highness's private papers this morning. I thought you'd like to have it." He held out a palm-size envelope, that she instantly recognized as bearing the crest and distinctive gold-edged design of the stationery used exclusively by her father.

A knot coiled in her stomach, part hope, part dread. Yet years of practice helped her retain an outward calm. "Thank you," she said, taking the missive from him. She waited, willing him to leave. When he didn't budge, she managed a cool smile. "Don't let me keep you. I'm sure you have other, more pressing duties to see to."

"How gracious of you to be concerned." Despite his words, he made no move to depart. "But before I take my leave, may I say how glad I am to see that the prince's death hasn't had an adverse effect on your enjoyment of the water?" His unblinking gaze didn't leave her face.

Catherine recoiled. Although the words were perfectly benign, the sentiment behind them was anything but, as was obvious from the chilly dislike in his eyes.

Then and there, she made a vow to speak to Daniel about the man's insufferable attitude. In the meantime, she lifted her chin and said with all the hauteur she could muster, "Leave me. Now."

For the briefest instant he looked surprised, and then he inclined his head. "As you wish." He made a cursory bow, turned and walked away.

She waited until he was out of sight, then slipped her finger under the envelope flap. She slid out the heavyweight piece of card stock. Her hands trembled slightly as she looked down and her father's distinctive handwriting jumped out at her.

Daughter,
I see no need for further discussion between us. Sadly, your decision to indulge your own desires rather than do your family duty doesn't surprise me. I will see to it your grandfather receives your regrets.

It was signed with Prince Marc's trademark looping *M*.

For a moment she couldn't seem to breathe. She'd been distraught when she believed her father had never received her e-mail message; now it appeared he had, but not only hadn't he cared, he'd continued to believe the worst of her, and oh, how it hurt.

It also served to revive her guilt: *she* should have been on the boat that day with King Thomas. If she had, perhaps she would have noticed something or somehow prevented the tragedy.

She suddenly could no longer contain her pain. She sagged back against a marble pillar and squeezed her eyes shut, fighting for control.

I will not cry. I will not. After all, this really isn't any great surprise. Father was angry; he hated having to dance attendance on Grandfather and clearly he wrote this before he had a chance to cool off and get over his pique. He didn't mean it, not really…

"Catherine? Has something happened?"

It took a moment for Kaj's concerned voice to penetrate her misery. Realizing how ridiculous she must appear, she straightened her spine and opened her eyes, doing her best to pull herself together. She dredged up a determined smile. "No, of course not."

"Then what's the matter?"

"It's nothing. I'm sorry I kept you waiting—"

"Don't," he said sharply. "Don't lie to me. Tell me. Now."

There was no mistaking his absolute determination to hear the truth. Still, she continued to resist, not entirely comfortable with sharing either her feelings or her problems. "Truly, Kaj, there's no need for you to be concerned."

His jaw hardened just for a second, and then his face abruptly softened. "Please." He reached out and lightly laid his palm against her cheek. "I'm not going away, nor do I intend to take no for an answer, so you may as well tell me what's upset you and be done with it."

His kindness nearly undid her. She swallowed, forcing down the tears suddenly clogging her throat as she conceded defeat. For all his gentle manner, it was clear he meant what he said. And she was in even less of a mood to argue with him than she had been with Gregor. Reluctantly she handed him the card.

He read through it in a handful of seconds, then looked at her questioningly.

She drew in a shaky breath and tried to put her thoughts in some sort of coherent order. "The day my father and grandfather died, I was supposed to be on the boat," she began. "Grandfather's eyesight was failing and I knew he didn't feel safe piloting the boat by himself anymore, but he was such a proud man. He absolutely refused to acknowledge that he needed help, so for several months I'd been going with him on one pretext or another.''

She couldn't contain a shaky sigh. ''But that day— that day I wasn't feeling well—I was suffering from some sort of nasty food poisoning—so I called Father and asked him to go in my place. He said he would, but it was obvious he wasn't happy about it, and before I could explain that I was ill, he accused me of being selfish, always thinking of myself, just like my mother. God forgive me, but I lost my temper. I told him he was absolutely right, that I was begging off because I had an absolutely essential appointment for a facial and manicure, and he—he hung up on me. The instant I heard the phone go dead, I realized how childishly I was behaving. I called him back but he wouldn't come to the phone, and as I was too indisposed to leave my room, I sent him an e-mail, asking if we might talk when he got back.

''This—'' she tapped the note card still in his hand ''—was his answer. His man Gregor, who's in charge of putting his affairs in order, apparently just found it.''

The line of Kaj's mouth had turned grim. Not at all certain what he was thinking, she turned to look blindly out at the last of the sunshine sparkling on the water. She cleared her throat. ''I should have been the one on the boat that day,'' she said, finally saying aloud what she'd been thinking for months. ''No matter how ill I felt, I was a better driver than Father. If only I'd been there—''

''That's nonsense,'' he interrupted harshly. ''For all you know, you would have been killed, too. You have to accept that accidents happen.''

"I'd like nothing better," she said fervently. "But it wasn't an accident."

"What? What do you mean?"

She felt his gaze sharpen but continued to stare out at the horizon. "At first we just assumed it was some terrible, unforeseen mishap. Then there was an attempt on Daniel's life in Chicago, and he and his family began to wonder. They hired an investigator, who's since found evidence the boat was sabotaged." Gathering her courage, she turned to face him. "Don't you see? If I'd been there, I might have seen something, or sensed that something was wrong—"

Looking into her anguished face, Kaj felt something fierce stir to life deep inside him. "And what if you hadn't?" he demanded, catching her by the arms and pulling her into the shelter of his body. "It would be you who was gone—and *that* is totally unacceptable to *me*."

In point of truth, while logically he could see that any ongoing threat most likely centered around Daniel and the succession, he felt a stab of anger that nobody had seen fit to even consider that Catherine might also be in danger, much less provide her with added protection.

Until now. Resolve hardened his voice. "What happened was not your fault," he said flatly. "It was a terrible thing, one we will talk about in greater detail in the future, but for now there's something else we need to discuss."

Clearly confused by his manner, not to mention the sudden change of subject, Catherine tipped her head back to directly meet his gaze, still looking pale and fragile from too much emotion. "And what is that?"

Her hair slid like silk against his hands; he ignored the instant stirring in his groin. "I have to leave for a few days. There are some things that demand my attention at home."

For the merest second her lips trembled, and then she got herself under control. "Oh."

He hesitated, but only for a moment. Cupping her chin in his hand, he stroked his thumb over her lips. "I don't want to go without you, Catherine. Come with me."

Seven

"**Y**ou're very quiet, *chaton*."

Taken aback by Kaj's observation, Catherine considered a moment, then realized it was true. She gestured at the view beyond the tinted glass limousine window as their driver negotiated the busy downtown streets of Akjeni, Walburaq's main city. "There's so much to take in."

That was a decided understatement. Everywhere she looked there was an eclectic mix of East and West, old and new. Shiny new high-rises pierced the azure sky several blocks away, while directly around her sprawled the low stone buildings of what Kaj called the Old City. Booths from a variety of small markets or *soukhs* crowded the side streets. As the limo slowed to negotiate around a donkey-powered cart, she glimpsed swatches of jewel-colored silks, the glitter of gold jewelry, vast stacks of baskets and piles of colorful rugs all in a single narrow alley.

And the crowds! Clustered on the narrow sidewalks, men in traditional white headdresses and the long white robes that Kaj called *dishdashas,* rubbed shoulders with men in European-style suits. Similarly, women wearing the newest New York and Paris fashions looked like bright butterflies as they flitted among their more conservatively attired, black *abaya*-wearing sisters with their modestly covered heads.

It was all very exotic, and for an instant she almost convinced herself what she'd told Kaj was the truth— that her silence stemmed from a preoccupation with her surroundings. Augmented, perhaps, by continuing distress about yesterday's encounter with Gregor Paulus.

Except, Catherine the princess had traveled the world and had seen far more startling sights than this prosperous and beautiful city. And Catherine the daughter had long known better than to allow her father's manservant to upset her.

More to the point, much as she might like to pretend otherwise, Catherine the woman knew that the true cause of her reticence was sitting right beside her.

She still found it hard to believe she'd actually confided in him the way she had yesterday afternoon. For as long as she could remember, even when her grandmother had been alive, she'd kept her own counsel. No matter what the provocation, the public Catherine always raised her chin and put on a show of regal indifference. Tears and fears, hurts and disappointments, even hopes and dreams, were handled alone, in private.

Until Kaj. From the moment he'd thrust himself into her path at Daniel and Erin's ball, he'd managed to get beneath her practiced reserve. And though she'd long recognized the power of his personality— it had been her primary reason initially for wanting to avoid him—in the past twenty-four hours she'd come to see that she'd underestimated his sheer charisma and commanding presence.

That had never been more evident than earlier today when they'd stepped aboard his private jet and set course for Walburaq. A subtle transformation had come over him. Although he'd been as polite and attentive to her as ever, there'd been a tone in his voice when he'd dealt with subordinates, a decisiveness about his every move, an ease of manner that had made her more aware than ever that he was accustomed to being in charge and enjoying instant obedience.

And though that was hardly a surprise, her reaction to the palpable power he exuded was. Not only was she even more hyperaware of him than usual, but for the first time in her life she also felt a desire to cede control, to lean into his big, hard body and simply let go.

It scared her to death. And excited her no end.

"Shall I turn down the air-conditioning?"

Kaj's concerned inquiry penetrated her musing. She turned to look at him. "What?"

"You're shivering. Are you cold?"

"Oh. No, I'm fine."

Despite her assurance, his concerned gaze swept over her like a lick of fire and her nipples promptly puckered. She felt them pressing against the lace of her bra and a splash of heat burned her cheeks since she knew very well her reaction had nothing to do with the temperature and everything to do with him.

In the next moment he seemed to realize it, too. Realized it, but still—thankfully—misunderstood.

He reached across the plush leather seat, captured her hand and brought it to rest against his muscled thigh. "It's all right, you know. Even here in Walburaq our agreement still stands. Nothing will happen between us without your express permission. However much—" his voice dropped ever so slightly, at odds with the twist of amusement that lurked at the corners of his mouth "—I might like to lock you in the seraglio and keep you solely for my pleasure."

"Seraglio?" Her lips parted in surprise. "You have a harem?"

He gave a theatrical sigh. "Yes—and no. I have the structure to house one, but not the requisite concubines. Fortunately—or unfortunately, depending on one's viewpoint—my great-grandmother put a stop to that."

"Really?" Grateful for any diversion to keep her mind off his proximity, she cocked her head. "How on earth did she manage that?"

His silvery eyes, so startling, framed by his inky lashes and bronze skin, warmed. "Her name was Anjouli, and the story goes that she was very young and very, very beautiful. She was also exceedingly clever and wise, and it is said that it took Khahil, my great-grandfather, a very long time to coax her into his bed. Once he finally did, he was entranced. So much so that when she eventually gave birth to his first son— until then he'd been blessed only with daughters—he impulsively told her he would give her anything her heart desired. I can't help but believe he thought she'd request her own palace or a trunkload of jewels, but instead she asked that he be hers exclusively. He agreed, and that—'' his teeth flashed in a rueful smile ''—set a precedent for future Russard sheikhs.''

His smile was irresistible and she answered it with one of her own. ''Oh, dear. Is that regret I hear?''

He shrugged, careless, elegant, infinitely masculine. ''I think not. Even without a harem, I've managed to acquire a more than adequate amount of carnal knowledge. Enough to know what—and whom—I want.'' Once more, his gaze played over her, then settled on her face, riveting her in place.

Another shiver went down her spine, and this time she didn't even attempt to deny that he was the cause. Yet some proud and obstinate part of her still wasn't quite ready to reveal the depth of her growing desire for him.

Not here, not now, not yet. Not when she still wasn't sure if she intended to act on what she felt or keep him to his word and make this trip a purely platonic one.

Doing her best to look thoughtful and nothing more, she nodded. ''I see.''

Outside, the city fell away and the road opened up. Fine white sand stretched in every direction, framed in the west by the aquamarine glimmer of sky meeting sea and to the east by the jagged upthrust of the Kaljar Hills.

After a score of miles, their driver turned onto a side road that climbed through a series of rising sand dunes. Eventually the road leveled out and in the near distance Catherine could see the brilliant green foliage of a large oasis, ringed by a cluster of buildings whose rooftops could be seen over a mammoth, crenellated wall. Behind them, soaring upward, was a storybook palace built of glistening white stone, with gilded domes and exquisitely shaped towers that looked as if it had been plucked from the pages of *1001 Arabian Nights*. "Oh, my," she murmured.

"Home," Kaj informed her, pride and affection unmistakable in his voice. "It's called Alf Ahkbar—which roughly means a thousand shades of green."

"I can see why."

Minutes later the limo swept through the compound's main gates, then slowed as it advanced down a narrow stone road set between a double row of chenar trees. Off to one side was a plaza where a spring bubbled up to fill a large, rectangular reflecting pool. Several dozen people, mostly women and children, looked up from various tasks, smiling and waving as the car went past.

The vehicle approached another set of gates, these fashioned of elaborate ironwork. Their driver spoke into the car phone, and the gate opened, then slid shut behind them. Five hundred feet later the limo pulled into a circular courtyard and came to a stop before the massive front doors of the palace itself.

Catherine drew in a deep breath as the full magnitude of her agreeing to come here sank in.

For the first time in her life she was alone with a man on his home ground. And she still didn't know what she wanted to do. Marriage, of course, remained out of the question. But did she really want to spend the rest of her life as a virgin?

* * *

A faint knock jarred Catherine awake. Blinking the
sleep from her eyes, she shifted on the azure velvet
divan, taking a moment to get her bearings.

The tiled ceiling overhead was ornate, decorated
with an intricate pattern of vines and flowers in shades
of turquoise, indigo and celadon green. Thick blue-
and-cream rugs covered the stone floor, and diaphanous silk panels lavishly embroidered with silver
thread draped the arched doorway that opened onto
the balcony. Matching silk panels encased the bed,
which boasted a delicately carved headboard inlaid
with lapis lazuli and a peacock-blue bedcovering scat-
tered with tasseled pillows in shades of green and
blue, amber, orchid and rose.

Unlike the more sedate furnishings of her rooms in
Altaria, the chamber was lush, playful and exotic, a
feast for the senses, and Catherine felt a return of the
delight she'd experienced when she'd first laid eyes
on it.

Which had been two hours ago, she realized with
a jolt as she glanced at her wristwatch. Appalled, she
sat up and swung her feet to the floor, doing her best
to quell her fascination with her surroundings and
force herself to think.

She remembered climbing out of the limousine, and
her surprise at the sweet scents of roses and jasmine
that had laced the crisp desert air. She recalled
crossing the courtyard and passing through a tall,
arched doorway. Once inside, she'd given a sigh of
pleasure at the lovely detail of the tile and latticework
walls, the tall ceilings and the cool serenity of the
interior that had greeted her. There had been a wide
staircase with shallow steps that climbed unhurriedly

up to a long gallery, a formal-looking reception area furnished with exquisite Georgian furniture to the left and a mirrored hallway dappled with shadows and sunlight to the right.

But it had been the view directly ahead of her that had most enchanted her. A series of carved arches had opened onto a shaded inner courtyard. Stands of bamboo had whispered beneath a nearly imperceptible breeze, while plants in enormous pots provided brilliant flowers in shades of magenta, scarlet, and lavender. Small, colorful birds darted among the foliage, and a peacock strutted along a paved path past a three-tiered fountain that was the courtyard's centerpiece.

It had been hushed, soothing and beautiful and Catherine had loved it on sight. She'd been nearly as entranced by the rest of the palace when Kaj had given her a quick tour. If she'd also felt relieved when he'd escorted her to her own quarters, tacitly revealing that he didn't expect her to share his room, well, that wasn't surprising given the current turbulence of her feelings. But it certainly did not excuse her lying down to rest for a few minutes and promptly sleeping away the afternoon—

Another knock at the door interrupted her musing. Positive it must be Kaj wondering what had become of her, Catherine shook off her languor, scrambled to her feet and raked her fingers through her hair. "Come in," she called, stepping forward as the door opened. "I'm so sorry—"

She broke off in confusion. In place of the tall, powerful figure she expected, there was a slim, pretty girl of perhaps fourteen. *"Masa'a alkhayr,"* the teen said, making a quick curtsy. "I am Sarab."

Catherine shifted gears, trying to remember some of the Arabic words she'd been studying. *"Marhaba, Sarab."* Hello.

The girl's dark, liquid eyes sparkled with interest. "You speak Arabic?" she asked.

Catherine shook her head. "No. Only a very little. I'm sorry."

"That is very much all right, Highness," the girl assured her. "Most fortunately, as you can surely tell, I speak the English very, very well. That is why my *jaddah* sent me to assist you."

"Jaddah?"

"My grandmother. She is the sheikh's…how do you say?…keeper."

Although she knew the choice of word certainly had to be a mistake, Catherine couldn't contain a smile. "Keeper?"

The girl nodded earnestly. "Yes. For many years now she has had the charge of the entire palace."

The pieces fell into place. "Ah. You mean house-keeper."

"Housekeeper, yes." Sarab nodded enthusiastically, then flashed Catherine another melting smile. "Please, I may come in?"

"Yes, of course." Stepping back out of the way, Catherine gestured for the girl to enter.

Sarab crossed the threshold, looked around and headed straight toward Catherine's suitcase, which lay open on a stand next to an enormous satinwood wardrobe inlaid with mother-of-pearl. She glanced politely at Catherine. "It is approved by you that I unpack your things?'' Catherine nodded, and the girl began the task, her slender fingers deft as she started to transfer clothes to the wardrobe's padded hangers.

Catherine watched, feeling strangely ill at ease. Although she'd lived her entire life surrounded by servants, she'd never known one so young, and it bothered her. "Have you worked for the sheikh long?'' she asked after a moment.

"Oh, no, Highness!'' The quick shake of the girl's head was accompanied by a small, amused giggle. "I'm just visiting while my parents attend a conference. They are doctors.'' Her pride was unmistakable. "My mother grew up here at Alf Ahkbar and has always been exceedingly clever, so Sheikh Kaj sent her to medical school as was her dream. He never forgets his people. He's a very great man, you know.''

This last was said with such reverence that Catherine was tempted to roll her eyes. Except that at the same time she felt a swell of something akin to pride.

Where on earth had that come from? she wondered, a little unnerved.

Sarab removed a stack of lacy lingerie from the suitcase. Holding the items as if they were made of cobwebs, she opened one of the wardrobe's drawers and laid them carefully inside. Worrying her lower lip, she appeared to ponder something, then turned to Catherine. "A thousand pardons, Highness, but... might I ask you a question?''

Even temporary help in Altaria knew better than to be so forward. Catherine parted her lips to say no, then hesitated. "Yes, I suppose,'' she said, her curiosity getting the better of her. Besides, it was better than trying to sort out the confusing mix of her feelings for Kaj.

"Are you going to marry the sheikh?"

So much for a diversion. "Why would you ask that?" she demanded.

Hot color tinged the girl's smooth cheeks. "Just…everyone is wondering. Sheikh Kaj has never brought a woman here, you see. He has a house in Akjeni where he…entertains. Not that I'm supposed to know that," she added hastily. "But you're so very beautiful and you seem so very nice, and Jaddah and my mother—all the village really—think it's time for him to settle down, even if one didn't have to consider Sheikh Tarik's most unfortunate will—" She broke off, her face growing even more flushed as she seemed to decide she'd now completely overstepped her bounds. "You do know about that, yes?"

There was nothing like having everyone know your business. Catherine felt a sudden sense of kinship with her host, as well as a perplexing protectiveness. "I believe the sheikh has mentioned it," she allowed.

Sarab continued to stare at her expectantly.

She lifted her chin. "As for the other, I haven't decided."

"But—" The girl swallowed whatever she'd been about to say, Catherine's cool tone apparently registering. She looked thoughtfully down at the open suitcase, then reached in and extracted two of the four negligees Catherine had impulsively brought with her, and placed them in the wardrobe. She delicately cleared her throat. "Sheikh Kaj is very handsome, is he not?"

"He is."

"And he would give you many pretty babies, yes?"

"Yes, I suppose."

"And he is generous and kind, brave and smart, tall and vigorous and very strong. He has much wealth and many beautiful homes and— Oh!" The girl's eyes rounded and her hand flew to her mouth. "Oh, no!"

Catherine jerked her thoughts away from the idea of having Kaj's baby, which she found absurdly appealing. "What on earth is the matter?"

"I forgot!" the girl wailed. "Jaddah said I was to tell you the sheikh would be most pleased if you'd honor him with your presence in the Peacock Garden. And I forgot!"

"Oh." Her initial alarm faded. "Is that all?"

"All? You cannot keep him waiting. He is the sheikh!" The teenager made a vague, shooing motion. "You must hurry!"

Catherine started to protest, then reconsidered as she took in the girl's very real distress. Her expression softened. She agreed, "I suppose I shouldn't keep him waiting."

Yet even as she allowed Sarab to lay out fresh clothes and help her with her hair, Catherine couldn't quell a prickle of amusement as the girl's words about making Kaj wait kept playing through her mind.

Poor Sarab, she thought wryly, if only she knew. Compared to what else I've been keeping Kaj waiting for, this is nothing.

But perhaps—just perhaps, since she still hadn't made up her mind—that was about to change.

* * *

Kaj stretched his legs, pleased to feel the familiar comfort of the fine white cotton of traditional Arab dress against his skin.

It was good to be home. Settling a little deeper into one of the oversize garden chairs in the inner courtyard, he soaked up the familiar sound of the soft splash of water from the fountain. He could hear the usual evening breeze blowing beyond the sheltered walls of the courtyard, but within the compound the flower-scented air was still. The only movement came from the scores of candle-filled lanterns illuminating the garden, their flickering light painting gilded shadows on walls and foliage.

The only thing more beautiful, he reflected, as he lifted his iced coffee and took an appreciative sip, was his company.

He regarded Catherine across the intimate width of their wrought-iron table-for-two. With her elegant bones, creamy skin and gleaming, shot-with-fire hair, he'd always considered her lovely. But tonight there was something different, something special about her. And after painstaking consideration, he'd finally figured out what.

"So." He took another sip of coffee. "Are you going to tell me what has you so amused?"

Her eyes widened slightly—but not before a telltale gleam of comprehension sparked in their emerald depths. "Pardon me?"

He unhurriedly set down his tall, narrow glass. "Ever since you joined me there's been the ghost of a smile lurking at the edges of your mouth. It was there all during dinner and dessert, it's continued to tantalize me as the sun has set and the moon has risen, it's teased at my senses during our every conversation I'd simply like to know if you're ever going to share its source with me.''

Her eyes gleamed mischievously. ''I don't know. I'm not sure that I should.''

Like a silken vise his desire for her tightened its hold on him.

He ignored it. Instinct told him that here, in what was indisputably his territory, it was more important than ever that *she* come to *him*. If keeping his hunger for her in check had also become a point of honor, an exercise in willpower that had his intellect pitted against his libido, so what? Eventually he *would* emerge the winner. ''And why is that?''

Her lips curved a fraction more. ''Perhaps because I think your ego is already more than healthy.''

He raised an eyebrow. ''You don't say.''

''I do. Although you've proven to be such a gracious host I suppose I might make an exception.''

''How generous of you.''

''Yes, isn't it?''

Their gazes locked. Again his body stirred, and again he disregarded it. He took another sip of coffee. ''Well?''

''Oh, all right.'' She gave an amused little sigh and made a production of crossing one leg over another. ''It appears you have a fan club.''

He told himself sternly not to notice the way the thin fabric of her dress clung to her rounded breasts and slim thighs. ''I do?''

''Mmm-hmm. Your housekeeper's granddaughter couldn't refrain from singing your praises.''

"Ah, Sarab. A lovely child. And exceedingly intelligent, too."

"You don't say?" She made no effort to hide the irony in her voice as she repeated his earlier words to him.

"But I do. What's more, I think it's extremely unkind of you to keep me in such suspense. What did she say?"

"I'm afraid I don't remember exactly." Her voice was airy. "Something about you being tall. And healthy, for someone your age. And I believe the word *handsome* may also have been used. But then, she *is* just a child."

The tartness of her humor pleased him. Too much. Suddenly restless, he came to his feet. "One with excellent taste," he said, stepping around the table and holding out his hand. "Come."

She was clearly puzzled by the abrupt change in his manner. "Where?"

"The moon is up. Let's take a walk."

To his gratification, she asked no further questions but pushed back her chair, took his hand and came to her feet, following his lead as he made his way to the far side of the garden and up a narrow set of stairs. He unlocked the gate at the top, and they stepped out onto the wall walk.

"Oh, Kaj," she murmured in an awestruck voice.

Bathed in pearlescent light, the desert seemed to stretch endlessly before them, still and silent except for the invisible play of the wind, while to the east a full moon lay low in an immense cobalt-blue sky. Not to be outdone, stars shimmered overhead, some spilled in swaths like vast rivers of sequins, some solitary and immense like the finest of diamonds.

It was breathtaking. But not half so much as Catherine's upturned face as she turned toward him, her eyes shining with reflected starlight. "It's beautiful. Absolutely beautiful."

There was something in her expression.... He tensed with anticipation, expecting her to come closer, to reach out and touch a hand to his arm or face or shoulder, to finally tell him she wanted him.

Instead, as their eyes met, her expression changed, transforming from warm delight to something he couldn't identify. Puzzled, he tried to put a name to what he was seeing—doubt, longing, chagrin? Before he could reach a conclusion, a trace of brilliant light streaked across the sky and Catherine hastily turned away to watch it. "A shooting star!" she exclaimed. "How perfect."

He considered her averted face and stiff spine. Whatever she felt, her body language spoke for itself. She may as well have donned a sign that said Don't Touch Me.

Frustration and what felt alarmingly like need roared through him. "I suppose it is," he managed.

She fixed her gaze on a distant spot, gingerly ran the tip of her tongue over her lower lip, then quietly ventured his name. "Kaj?"

"What?"

"Thank you for asking me here. For being—" she paused, as if searching for just the right words "—such a good friend."

Friend? She couldn't mean it. What about *lover?* He clenched his jaw, excruciatingly aware the cotton pants that had been loose earlier in the evening now felt damnably confining—a ridiculous state of affairs for a man of his age and experience.

"A ridiculous state of affairs, period," he could just imagine his cousin Joffrey drawling in his usual amused way.

The thought of what else his relative would have to say about the current situation made him grimace. Yet it also served to remind him of what was at stake. He wanted Catherine to be his wife, not just a one-night stand.

And not because he had designs on Joff's painting, he thought impatiently. But because he was now more convinced than ever that she was the perfect choice for him. She was smart, interesting and beautiful, generous of heart but nobody's pushover. He had every confidence she'd be a caring mother to his children, a thoughtful and responsible guardian of his people, a gracious hostess, an asset to his varied business dealings. She was clearly not inclined toward promiscuity, but still spirited enough that he doubted he'd ever suffer from boredom.

And hadn't he learned by watching his parents the incalculable value of making a well-thought-out match, of never letting his body or emotions overrule his common sense?

Of course he had.

He slowly let out his breath. "I'm honored to be your friend, *chaton*. Thank you." Bracing himself against the increased desire that touching her, no matter how innocently, always brought him, he reached out and clasped her small, elegant hand. "Come. I'll take you to your room. It's been a long day and you must be tired.''

She parted her lips as if to protest, then appeared to think better of it. ''I suppose you're right,'' she said in a subdued voice.

By way of an answer he walked over and opened the gate, indicating with a flourish of his hand that she should precede him down the stairs. Avoiding his gaze, she did as asked. Congratulating himself on his self-control, he closed the gate and started after her.

And that was when he discovered his mistake. All it took was one look at the firm, rounded cheeks of her derriere flexing beneath her thin dress to send his testosterone level soaring again.

Scowling, he flicked a baleful glance at the heavens, knowing he was doomed to spend yet another restless night alone.

Eight

Coward.

Catherine paced her bedroom, her self-condemnation gaining ground as she replayed her exchange with Kaj over and over.

Despite what some of the men in her past had assumed, her virginity didn't make her either naive or unworldly. And while she was currently of the opinion that that didn't always qualify as an advantage, she still couldn't escape the truth: the moment she'd stepped into the courtyard tonight and seen Kaj sitting there, something inside her had shifted and she'd known he was the one she wanted to be her "first."

The reasons then—as now—seemed obvious. She admired how comfortable he was in his own skin, the way he could be commanding without being a bully, the fact that he could make her laugh. She liked his strength and tenacity, his willingness to stand up to her, his wry sense of humor. She cherished his unexpected kindnesses and respected his honesty.

Young Sarab had gotten it right when she'd said he was a good man.

That he was also heartbreakingly handsome and wonderfully exotic Catherine had always known. But seeing him this evening, dressed as befitted the Arab half of his heritage, so clearly at ease with himself and so assured of his masculinity, she'd also realized how tired she was of fighting her attraction to him.

So she'd let down her guard just as she had after her encounter with Gregor. Only this time instead of telling Kaj her troubles, she'd given herself permission to reveal her softer, more playful side. She'd done her best to make sure he knew she was enjoying herself. And that she enjoyed being with him.

And everything had gone well—until the time to speak up had come and she'd faced the prospect of admitting she'd changed her mind, that she wanted him in every way the word *want* could be defined. Looking up at him, her fingers tingling with the urge to touch him, to brush back a stray strand of his glossy black hair, to trace the line of his eyebrow, to explore the muscular contours of his chest, she'd panicked. Not only hadn't she confessed she wanted to make love with him, she'd actually thanked him for being her friend.

Just thinking about it made her wince.

In stark contrast to her sorry performance, Kaj had been an absolute gentleman, not pressing her to deliver what they'd both known she'd been promising.

Which might not have been so bad if she hadn't clearly seen both the desire, the surprise and the disappointment in his eyes in the moment she'd lost her nerve and turned away.

But she had. And she couldn't get his expression out of her mind. Making matters worse, no matter how many times she went over it, she didn't understand why she'd behaved as she had. After all, her decision to have sex with Kaj hadn't been a sudden whim. Over the years she'd known plenty of attractive men but had never felt the slightest urge to share her body with any of them. Yet, where Kaj was concerned, one way or another she'd been thinking of nothing else ever since they met.

So why, why, *why,* having finally made a decision, had she acted the way she had?

Restless, uneasy, agitated, she reached the far end of the room. She started to turn to retrace her path, only to freeze as she caught sight of her shadowy reflection in the mirrored wall of the bathroom a dozen feet away.

Her long, nearly transparent silk robe of peach, pale-green and cream clung to her bare shoulders. The flimsy garment did nothing to hide the way her ice-green satin nightgown molded to her high breasts or rounded hips or the long line of her thighs. Her hair was tumbled around her shoulders, her cheeks were flushed, her lower lip plump and swollen from being gnawed on.

She looked like a woman who'd just rolled out of her lover's bed. Or a woman in a fever to climb in....

She whirled away, unable to bear her own image, much less the ideas it provoked. Pacing back the way she'd come, she felt as if she couldn't breathe. Her heart began to pound; her skin felt tight; the walls seemed to close in, making the same space that earlier had been such a source of pleasure now feel like a gilded cage.

Unable to stand it a moment longer, she fled toward the balcony, threw open the French doors, took a half dozen steps outside—and just as suddenly jerked to a halt, sucking in what little breath she had left.

Twenty-five feet to her right stood Kaj, his head bowed, his back to her, his hands braced against the parapet. He was barefoot and naked from the waist up, and, despite the distance between them, thanks to the moonlight she could see the muscles in his wide shoulders and lean waist bunch with every slight shift of his weight.

Her stomach hollowed. Her throat went dry and she felt a sudden throbbing at the apex of her thighs. Most alarming of all, however, was the way her heart squeezed at the tension of his posture.

In a burst of clarity, she understood what she'd refused to face only minutes earlier.

She cared about him. More than she'd ever cared about another person. Enough that earlier tonight some self-protective part of her had made one last desperate attempt to keep him at arm's length and keep her heart safe. Enough that the only word powerful and exclusive enough to describe what she felt was...*love*.

She remained stock-still as the idea washed through her, half expecting her sanity to return and tell her to stop being ridiculous. She didn't love Kaj. She couldn't. Hadn't she long ago decided that love wasn't for her?

Yet as the seconds ticked by, as the sensual play of the wind cooled her cheeks, tugged at her hair and ruffled her gown, her inner voice remained silent. With a growing sense of wonder, she realized that loving Kaj al bin Russard simply felt…right. That this time there were no doubts.

She wasn't sure how long she stood watching him, her heart hammering in her chest, her throat tight, her eyes stinging with her newly realized feelings.

But eventually, watching him wasn't nearly enough, while the need to touch him became overwhelming.

She began to walk, drawn to him like a compass to true north. Desire beckoned, tempting her to keep going until she was pressed against his gleaming bronzed back. Only her sense of fair play held her back, insisting he deserved something more.

Something better.

She stopped when a mere arm's length separated them. "Kaj."

His head jerked up. Although only an instant passed before he swiveled around on the balls of his feet, she was so attuned to him she saw the slight shudder that went through him before he turned. Nevertheless, he didn't look happy to see her. "What are you doing out here?"

Raising her chin, she stood her ground. "I need to tell you something."

He was shaking his head even before she finished. "Whatever it is, I'm sure it can wait until morning."

She might have been discouraged if not for the

sheen of perspiration suddenly sleeking his skin, the tautness rippling his abdomen, the effort he had to make to control his breathing as his gaze flicked over her. Despite his attempt to convince her otherwise, he was anything but indifferent to her. "No," she said softly. "I don't think so."

Impatience flashed across his face. "Catherine—"

She stepped close enough to reach up and press her fingers to his mouth. "I want you, Kaj. Make love to me."

He went still as a statue. His eyes locked on hers, not wavering even as she allowed herself the luxury of stroking the strong line of his jaw.

He cleared his throat. "What did you say?"

"Make love to me. Teach me how to make love to you."

For another second he remained anchored in place. Then he slowly let out his breath, looped his hands around her waist and tugged her close. "Damn. I was beginning to think you'd never ask." Bending his head, he covered her mouth with his own.

Magic. Madness. Bliss. Her body seemed to melt like a candle overrun by a forest fire. She molded herself against him, exulting in the satin-over-bronze texture of his skin, the flat planes and rounded curves of muscle in his chest and arms, the sleek power of his legs as he pulled her into the cradle of his thighs.

He became her universe. His breath fed her lungs, his strength held her up, the beat of his heart dictated the rhythm of her own. A rhythm that began to race as he slid his hands lower and gently squeezed the sensitive curve of her bottom.

She whimpered and pressed even closer.

His mouth still fused to hers, he swept her off her feet and into his arms. She vaguely registered that he was carrying her somewhere, but it didn't matter. What did was the delicious heat of his tongue tangled with hers, the sweet sensation of having one of his hands press the side of her breast while the other cupped her hip. Then there was the way the swelling ridge of his erection pushed against her with his every step.

Angling sideways, they passed through a doorway. Surprised by the faint smell of sandlewood and cloves, she broke the seal of their mouths, lifted her head and looked around.

She knew immediately she was in Kaj's bedroom. It was larger than her room and more lavishly decorated, the walls embedded with bands of gold and silver tiles in a diamond pattern. An opulent rug covered most of a pale marble floor. She had an impression of dark gleaming furniture, dimly realized the soft, exotic music she heard was spilling from hidden speakers and that the scents that had first caught her attention were coming from a dozen glowing candles grouped together in a wall niche.

But it was the oversize bed that quickly became her focus. Backed by a massive headboard of gold and silver latticework, it was framed by gold cloth drapes that swept to the floor. The matching satin comforter lay folded across the bed's foot, exposing rich black sheets. The effect was uncompromisingly masculine and breathtakingly handsome.

Which perfectly described the master of Alf Ahkbar, she thought, her gaze swinging back to Kaj as he set her on feet. Cupping her face in his palm, he brushed his lips over her cheeks, jaw and brow. "You're sure?"

Tenderness flooded her. For all that his voice sounded calm, she felt the slight tremor in his hand. "Yes."

"Very well." He took a half step back, unwound the band of fabric at his waist and stepped out of his pants. Her breath lodged in her throat as his erection sprang free and she had her first unobstructed view of what a real man looked like.

Massive. Impressive. Impossible. The thoughts tumbled through her mind a little hysterically before her reason reasserted itself. After all, men and women had been procreating for untold centuries, she reminded herself, and everyone seemed to survive. At least everyone she'd ever known.

Then Kaj slid her robe off her shoulders and her gown over her head, and her thoughts fragmented yet again as she glanced up to find *him* looking at *her*. Too aroused to be self-conscious, she watched, flattered and fascinated as the skin across his nose and cheekbones drew tight at the same time a muscle ticked to life in his jaw.

"Ah, princess... Do you know how beautiful you are? How perfect?" He brushed the pad of his thumb across the straining tip of her left nipple. "How much I hunger to make you mine?"

His thumb strafed her tender flesh again and her knees nearly buckled. Instinctively she stepped forward to clutch his broad shoulders for support, only to shiver as she felt his thick masculine length press firmly against her stomach. "As a matter of fact—" she did her best to ignore the heat she felt rising into her cheeks "—I believe I do." She pressed a kiss to the shallow valley between his pectoral muscles.

His response was midway between a groan and a chuckle. Gently weaving his hands into her hair, he tipped her face up to his. "Why do I suddenly have the feeling you're going to make me as crazy in bed as you do out of it?"

"I can't imagine. Perhaps because you're beginning to know me?"

Although her words were lightly spoken, as he looked down at her his amusement drained away. "Yes," he said, slowly running his thumbs over the curve of her cheekbones to frame her mouth. "I think perhaps I am." With that he leaned down and once more began to kiss her.

The play of his lips was even more drugging than before. A fever of need seemed to spread through her, and instinctively she locked her arms around his neck and hoisted herself up, wrapping her legs around his hips.

Her action obviously surprised him; for a moment his whole body stilled. Then he made a fierce sound low in his throat and wrapped an arm beneath her to brace her, lifting her higher and deepening the kiss.

She felt the broad tip of his staff nudge against her at the same time his tongue stabbed possessively into her mouth. Excitement, anticipation and need went from bud to blossom, deepening the ache pulsing at her center. "Kaj. Yes. Oh, yes." Loosening her hold on his neck, she sank down and felt him slip shallowly inside her.

"Catherine, darling, slow down. I don't want to hurt you."

"You won't," she assured him breathlessly. "You couldn't. I want you, Kaj. Inside me. Now." Trembling, she wrestled the tie out of his hair, thrust her hands into the thick, inky locks and dragged his head to hers. "Please." Copying his action of a moment earlier, she breached his mouth with her tongue and mimicked the slow thrusting motion that had set her own blood on fire.

He made a strangled sound of protest. Or was it surrender? The answer came as he abruptly tightened his hold on her and flexed his powerful hips.

Catherine felt a brief, unexpected flash of pain as he slid deeper, then a stinging discomfort as her body stretched to accommodate him. The latter was more than bearable, however, offset as it was with other sensations: the drugging warmth of his lips plying hers, the delicious friction of her nipples rubbing against his hard chest, the unexpected sense of security she felt being in his arms. "More," she urged impatiently.

A shudder passed through him, shaking them both. Then he bent his knees and pushed.

The slow slide of him inside her seemed to last forever and left them both out of breath and trembling. Fully buried, he dragged his mouth away from hers to brush kisses over her cheeks and eyes. "Are you all right?" he murmured.

"Mmm," she answered, her focus inward. "Don't stop."

"No. I won't." Shifting his hold on her, he pulled back slightly, then rocked his hips.

It was like dragging a match over a strike strip. Heat flickered, expanded, flared. It was only a tiny flame at first. Until he repeated the motion. And then she caught fire. "Oh!"

Again he moved, settling into a steady pumping rhythm that soon had her rocking back.

"Kaj."

"What?"

"It's not—" She sucked in air, her voice shaking. "It's not enough. I want...I need...you. Deeper. Harder."

"Aw, Catherine. Sweetheart, you're killing me." Tightening his grip on her to keep them joined, he walked toward the bed, where, the muscles bulging in his upper arms, he slowly lowered her until her upper body rested on the high mattress.

Bracing his legs, he pulled back until he was almost out of her. Automatically she tightened the lock of her legs on his waist. "Kaj, please—"

"Shh." To her disbelief, instead of immediately acquiescing to her plea as she expected, he shifted his hands so that one supported her bottom while the other slid over the top of her thigh. Then one big finger skated sideways, zeroed in on the swollen seat of her need and rubbed. She cried out in shocked pleasure, and that was when he drove forward.

For one mind-altering moment the world ceased to exist as she knew it. Her stomach hollowed, her skin flushed, her back bowed, her every muscle clenched as she was swept by a monumental explosion of pleasure.

Powerless against such hot, mindless delight, she felt herself tighten around Kaj as he pumped full into her. He gave a guttural shout, then she too was again crying out as a second, even stronger explosion rocked her.

Catherine gladly bore his considerable weight when he collapsed on top of her moments later. And she knew, even as he wrapped his arms around her, keeping her close as he rolled onto his side, that nothing in her life would ever be the same.

Kaj lay sprawled in the center of the bed, one hand tucked beneath his head, watching with lazy interest as fingers of sunshine reached through the window tops to paint shimmering golden stripes on the ceiling overhead.

He felt boneless. Satiated. Beyond content. But then hours and hours of incredible sex with an incredible woman could do that to a man.

He shifted to look at Catherine. She lay nestled against him, her head cradled on his shoulder, her arm draped across his chest, her fingers lightly tracing the path from his ear to his collarbone. Although she'd stirred awake some twenty minutes ago, they had yet to speak. There was no need since their shared silence was so comfortable they might have been lovers for years.

Kaj had never experienced anything like it. Or like the night they'd just shared. His hunger for her had seemed to grow as the hours passed. Their every kiss, every touch, every joining had only made him want to hold her closer, thrust himself deeper, feel her shudder and cry out yet another time. And though he'd managed to cling to some semblance of control, to leash his strength so he wouldn't hurt her, he hadn't been able to stop. He doubted they'd slept an entire hour altogether.

Which might have concerned him far more were it not for the fact that, as often as not, it had been Catherine who'd initiated another round of lovemaking. She was definitely unique, a jewel to be treasured, he thought, idly rubbing his thumb over the silken skin of her hip. "Good morning, princess."

Her fingers stilled and she angled her head up toward him. "Good morning yourself," she said softly.

"How do you feel?"

"Tired. Marvelous." She gave a small, delicate yawn. "What about you?"

"Me?" He considered. "As if I just ran the world's longest marathon." He smiled. "And won."

She smiled back, and he realized she looked different. For the first time since they'd met she'd lost her usually guarded expression.

The discovery made him feel even more protective and territorial than usual, and he gathered her even closer. "I've pictured you here, in my bed, you know. I imagined the way you'd look against these very sheets, with your white skin and Titian hair. But my imagination didn't begin to do you justice."

"Oh." Pleasure colored her cheeks, but she glanced away from him and ran her hand over the exquisitely soft fabric that draped their hips. "*I* never imagined black velvet sheets. I always thought satin sheets would be the preferred choice for…worldly pursuits."

He shook his head. "No. Satin feels either too hot or too cold. Plus it's slippery."

"Ah." She considered a moment, then nodded thoughtfully. "No traction. A definite drawback."

His lips twitched at her serious tone. "My, aren't you a quick study."

"I suppose I am." She shifted to look at him. "Is that a problem?"

"Absolutely not. Your intelligence is one of the reasons I chose you to be my wife."

For a long moment she was silent. Then she said with a touch of amusement as well as something else he couldn't quite identify coloring her voice, "Do you know, sheikh, I remember agreeing to a lot of things last night. But a marriage proposal wasn't one of them."

He twisted a lock of her hair around his finger. "I rather imagine that's because I was too busy with other things to ask. But I will. And when I do, you'll say yes."

You'd better. Because you're mine, sweet Catherine, in every way that matters. And I intend to keep it that way.

The sudden violence of his emotions caught him by surprise, and he felt an abrupt stab of uneasiness.

He promptly shrugged it off. After all, he'd already acknowledged she inspired a host of unique feelings in him: possessiveness, protectiveness, an unprecedented tenderness. Just as he'd admitted that, though he didn't love her, he cared about her in ways he'd never cared about another woman. The fact that he wanted to please her, to make her happy, was a miracle all by itself.

A miracle that should help ensure that theirs would

be a successful marriage. "Trust me, *chaton*. We're meant to be together."

Her face softened, but to his surprise all she said was, "I'll think about it."

As responses went, it was totally unacceptable, and for one very long moment he was tempted to press the issue, to do whatever it took to bend her to his will. He hadn't a doubt that if he put his mind to it he could make her give him the answer he desired.

Yet, after a bit more thought, he realized such a power play was unnecessary. Given what had occurred between them in the past twelve hours, it was obvious she had deep feelings for him. All he had to do was be patient and she was bound to come around to his way of thinking and see the advantages of a union between them.

The realization sent a surge of energy through him. "Very well. In the meantime—" gently shifting her off him he climbed out of bed "—it occurs to me there's someone you should meet."

"You can't be serious."

"Oh, but I am."

Yawning again, she made a shooing motion. "You go ahead. Visit whomever you like." She snuggled deeper into the bed. "I'll stay here. I'm afraid I'm not in the mood to make conversation."

"That's quite all right. My friend isn't big on talk."

"Kaj—"

He held out his hand. "Please?"

Her gaze touched his proffered hand, took a leisurely dip lower, then slowly rose to his face. She chewed her full bottom lip. "Would we shower first?"

Given that he was once again as hard as a rock, it seemed like an excellent idea. "Yes."

"In that case..." She tossed off the covers and reached for him.

Nine

"So?" Kaj stood next to his friend, one hand resting on the big fellow's muscular shoulder. "What do you think?"

"Are you serious?" Catherine stared in awe at the huge orange tiger, who from whiskers to tail had to measure over nine feet long. "He's incredible. And utterly beautiful."

Kaj cocked his head. "You sound surprised. Did you think I was making things up that day at the orphanage when I told the children about him?"

"I wasn't sure," she admitted.

He made a faint tsking sound. "You need to have more faith in me, *chaton*. Although I've been known to withhold information during business negotiations on occasion, I don't lie. And certainly not to children."

"Yes. I know that. Now."

"Good. Now come say hello to Sahbak. Like me, he has a penchant for beautiful, red-haired women."

She didn't hesitate to do as he bade. Partly because she'd been raised to always show courage when confronted with a challenge. But also because she trusted Kaj not to put her in danger. Moving forward to stand at his side, she offered her hand to the big cat to be sniffed.

"Have you known that many?" The words popped out of her mouth before she could stop them.

"What? Redheads?" He gave her a lazy smile that made her feel warm all over. "Personally, just one. Sahbak, however, is acquainted with a number of such ladies. Although the captive Amur tiger population is considered to be stable, his genes are still very much in demand."

"I've never heard of Amur tigers."

"You've probably heard them referred to as Siberian tigers."

"I thought Siberian tigers were white."

"No, those are actually Indian tigers."

She rolled her eyes, and without warning, Sahbak took a friendly swipe at her hand with his long pink tongue. It was not unlike being stropped by a damp emery board and she gave a slight start. "Oh!"

"He likes you." There was no mistaking the satisfaction in Kaj's voice. "Good."

"You make it sound as if I've passed some sort of test." She tried not to sound as pleased as she felt as the cat licked her again.

"I'd say you have." Kaj scratched behind the animal's rounded ears, and the beast promptly began to make a low rumbling noise that was clearly the tiger version of purring. "After all, we've known each other a long time, he and I. I was just seventeen and he was a mere cub when he was given as a gift to my father. He's usually quite a good judge of character."

Unable to help herself, she rubbed her hand over the ruff of white fur that encircled the tiger's neck. "Then perhaps you won't be offended if I tell you I'm not sure I approve of an individual person, rather than a zoo, having this kind of animal. In Altaria, trading or owning any sort of endangered species is illegal."

"As it should be everywhere, since there are less than a thousand Amurs left, wild and captive. But the man who acquired Sahbak as a cub has never concerned himself with legalities, no matter the country, much less cared about wildlife conservation. And my father always believed *he* was a law unto himself. It took me several years just to convince him to have Sahbak's name entered in the International Tiger Studbook, and he only agreed then because he knew no one could force him to give the tiger up."

"Your father sounds rather difficult."

"My father was impossible," Kaj said simply. "He could be charming when he chose, and he did have some qualities I admired, but the majority of the time he wasn't an easy man to be around, particularly in the latter years of his life. He had to be in control, and he was willing to do whatever it took to get his own way."

Catherine reached out and touched her hand to his arm. "I'm sorry."

The strain on his face abruptly vanished. "Yes, I know you are. And while it's not very noble of me, it's a relief that you understand. Which is another example of why we're so well suited."

"Now, sheikh," she admonished, amused by how quickly his mood had turned around, "let's not ruin a perfectly lovely afternoon by bringing that up again. I told you I'd think about us. And I will."

With a wry smile he squeezed her hand. "Very well. But in an attempt to redeem the family image, allow me to at least explain that, except for a female with cubs, tigers are by nature solitary creatures. They don't do well in groups, which can put a real strain on zoos and other captive habitats. Because of that, and because I have the resources to provide a very large and customized enclosure, Sahbak is better off here than he would be any number of other places."

"He certainly appears to think so." She watched as the tiger, apparently tired of all their talk, leaned against Kaj and nudged the sheikh with his large head, clearly impatient to be petted again.

Ever dutiful, Kaj again began to scratch between the animal's ears, although he had to strain to stay on his feet as the contented beast slouched more and more against him.

"How much does he weigh?" Catherine asked curiously.

"Six hundred sixty pounds. And at the moment—" with a grunt, he gave the tiger's shoulder a shove that seemed to affect the placid Sahbak not at all "—I'm feeling every one of them. Lazy bounder."

"Pardon, Mr. Kaj." They both looked over as the younger of the two men Kaj had introduced as the tiger's caretakers spoke up from just outside the enclosure gate. "You have a phone call. Mrs. Siyadi transferred it from the main house to the office here. She says to tell you it's the call you've been expecting."

"Thank you, Jamal," Kaj answered. "I'll be right there." He motioned to Saeed, the other handler, who'd been quietly standing vigil several yards away, poised to intervene if the big cat made any unexpected moves. "If you'd be so kind as to take over. Sahbak seems to have a number of itches that need to be scratched."

"Certainly, sir." Walking slowly, Saeed went to stand opposite Kaj and began to knead the animal's neck. Snuffling happily, Sahbak shifted his weight toward the source of this new pleasure, barely taking note as Catherine and Kaj made their way out of the enclosure.

Clasping Catherine's hand, Kaj interlaced their fingers as they walked up the slight hill toward the airy stone structure that housed Alf Ahkbar's stables. "Praise be for phones," he said dryly. "Another few minutes and Sahbak would have been on top of me. An experience I've had previously and would prefer not to repeat."

"Did he hurt you?"

"Only my dignity. But being a tiger's doormat is not the image I want you to have of me."

There was slight chance of that, Catherine thought wryly, her pulse racing merely from the innocent contact of their fingers.

But then, where Kaj was concerned, she seemed to be ultrasensitive in all sorts of odd places—the backs of her knees, ears and neck, the inside of her wrists, the bottom of her feet—that until last night she'd never considered erogenous zones.

Even more confounding, her lips and breasts, as well as the inside of her thighs, actually ached. And not from being tender or tired as might be expected. No, they ached for *more*.

For the first time in her life she understood what it was to hunger for a man. To hunger for Kaj.

Coming on the heels of last night, it surprised her. She'd just assumed that once they made love the sharpest edge of her desire for him would be dulled. That she'd feel relaxed and fulfilled. That the compulsion to be close to him would ease and that the little things like a warm look from him or a husky tone in his voice would lose their power to affect her.

Clearly that hadn't happened. And didn't seem likely to in the immediate future.

Kaj let go of her hand and motioned for her to precede him into the large, air-conditioned office just inside the stable block. "This should only take a second," he promised, giving her arm one last, proprietary squeeze. Moving across the well-appointed space, he propped a hip on top of a large, curved desk, turned the phone around, put the receiver to his ear and punched a button. "Russard."

She looked around, taking note of the state-of-the-art computer workstation, the floor-to-ceiling stainless steel file cabinets, the inviting seating area that occupied the room's near corner. But it was the display of framed photos on the far wall that drew her. To her delight, a closer inspection proved that although most of the pictures were of horses, Kaj also appeared in some of them.

In one he couldn't have been more than two or three. Nevertheless he sat proudly atop a lovely dapple gray mare, a smile of unabashed delight warming his small face. Even then he appeared to have a light grip on the reins.

In another he was perhaps five years older. His face was thinner, his body long and rangy, his expression oddly guarded for someone his age. All of the joy that was so evident in the first photo was gone.

In the next several shots there was again a jump of several years. But to her relief, in these he appeared happy again, something she attributed to his company—a smaller boy with gilt hair and an impish smile who could only be his cousin Joffrey.

Smiling, she admired a teenage Kaj and his horse done up in full native regalia, caught her breath at a shot of him in formal English hunting attire atop a big bay taking an enormous cross-country fence, nodded her approval as he was caught leaning down to accept a blue ribbon and silver plate atop the same horse.

Next on the wall were several snapshots of him as a tall, elegant youth on the cusp of manhood, a tiger cub that had to be a young Sahbak in his arms. There was also a larger, more formal picture, this one with a man who had to be Kaj's father, and the cub. Boldly inscribed across the bottom in black ink was an inscription.

"My dear sheikh. May my humble gift to you grow to be as noble and fierce as his new master. Your servant, The Duke."

She frowned, disturbed but not certain why. Something about that last seemed almost familiar....

"Catherine? Is something the matter?"

With a start, she realized Kaj was standing beside her. "No. I don't think so."

"Then why are you frowning so?"

"It's just that this picture..." She trailed off, feeling silly. Surely the use of that title was just a coincidence. Lord knew there were lots of dukes in the world.

"What about it?"

"Do you know the man who wrote this?" She indicated the inscription.

"I know him, yes. His name is Georges Duclos. The other is an appellation I'm sure he gave himself."

"He's not a real duke?"

He grimaced. "No."

"What does he do?"

He gave her a puzzled look. "Why do you want to know?"

"I just do."

He considered her a moment longer, then sighed, no doubt at the determination that most likely was stamped on her face. "Very well. If it's important to you. The duke is a middleman of sorts. He made a vast fortune as an illegal arms broker in the 1980s, then retired and did his best to become part of the so-called jet set, befriending a number of influential European and Arabic royalty.

"Because he still had criminal contacts and a total lack of scruples, he gained a reputation as a fixer, if you will. He was—and is—someone who can provide a prominent, married friend with the name of a person willing to put a scare into an ex-girlfriend who threatens to go to the tabloids, for instance. Conversely, he's also been known to connect a wealthy crime lord who wishes to see a certain law watered down or eliminated altogether with a down-on-his-luck but still-well-connected aristocrat.''

Catherine turned to stare blankly at the photo as she digested what he was telling her. "I see."

Kaj laid his hand on her shoulder. "Now tell me why he's of interest to you."

"It's probably nothing, just a coincidence. But a few weeks ago I used my father's computer to check his e-mail. I was trying to see if he'd read my message, the one I told you about. More to the point, there was another e-mail. I don't remember the exact wording, but in essence it assured my father that things were in order and that as long as something continued to go on unhindered, a loan he'd taken out would be retired.

"I honestly didn't think much of it at the time, since my father often did favors for people and I'd only recently learned he owed a great deal of money, and I had...other things on my mind. But I do remember it was signed exactly the way your photo is: 'Your servant, The Duke.'" Ignoring the sick feeling twisting through her stomach, she forced herself to meet Kaj's gaze without flinching. "The more I consider it, the more likely it seems that your duke and mine could be the same man."

"Yes." Kaj's voice was unexpectedly gentle. "I think you're right."

They both fell silent, considering.

Catherine was the first to speak. "Given this Duclos's reputation and the kind of people he knows…" She swallowed. "Do you think he could have anything to do with what happened to Grandfather's boat? Or the attempt on Daniel's life?"

Kaj shook his head. "Doubtful. Or at least, not personally. Remember, he always acts merely as a middleman. As for the third party he was representing, if you're accurately remembering what was in that e-mail, it sounds as if everything was under control. Why would anyone commit murder if they didn't have to?"

"Yes, I suppose that's true."

"In any event, when we get back to Altaria we can make a hard copy of the e-mail and let the king and his people take it from there. That is, if that's all right with you?"

"It's fine." It was more than that, really. Having someone she could confide in, whose judgment she trusted and who treated her like an intelligent partner, was a rare and precious gift.

"Now, quit worrying." Wrapping an arm around her shoulders, Kaj drew her toward the door. "This will all work out, I promise you, although it may take some time to get all the answers."

They stepped into the stable aisle, and as if there to provide a distraction, a good two dozen priceless Arabian horses, their necks extended over the bottom halves of their stall doors, nickered as they caught sight of Kaj.

Catherine raised her eyebrows. "My, you're popular. Let me guess—these are all mares."

"Of course not." He gave her a smug, supercilious look that was so unlike him she had to choke back a laugh. "Such is the strength of my appeal that I'm appreciated by all of my horses."

She did laugh then. "Oh, really? I don't suppose it could have something to do with the carrots you were handing out earlier?"

"Certainly not." Pulling her close to his side so they were pressed hip to thigh, he urged her toward the end of the corridor. "Now enough of this nonsense. We're falling behind schedule."

"We have a schedule?"

"Yes."

"I don't suppose you'd be willing to share it with me?"

"But, of course. First we're going to eat the lovely late lunch Mrs. Siyadi has prepared for us. Then I think we could both use a nap so we'll be well rested for tonight."

"What are we doing tonight?"

"Now that, *chaton,* I can't tell you. After all—" he swung her around, planted a kiss on her lips, then pulled quickly away, a devilish glint in his smoky-gray eyes "—if I did, it wouldn't be a surprise."

Kaj pulled the blindfold loose from Catherine's face and took a step back.

He watched with a now familiar combination of tenderness, expectation and lust as she made a slow circle, her long legs flexing in her high, spike heels, her body slim and supple beneath her thin blue sheath. She took her time, examining every detail of her surroundings.

The tiny oasis, with its handful of palm trees and its deep crystalline pool. The pair of glossy-coated horses and the stacks of supplies he'd had brought in so he and Catherine might stay as long as it suited them.

The airy pavilion, draped with silken hangings, lit against the night by dozens of hanging brass lanterns. The priceless jewel-toned carpets piled to create a floor over the soft sand. The large *dawashak,* or mattress, covered in dozens of pillows.

And surrounding everything, for as far as the eye could see, the desert. Empty. Mysterious. Eternal.

By the time Catherine's gaze finally came to rest on him, her beautiful green eyes were wide and awestruck. "I feel as if I've stepped into a dream," she said softly.

"You're not disappointed we didn't go into Akjeni to sample the nightlife, then?" He'd been afraid after he'd assisted her into the Land Rover instead of the limo that, blindfolded or not, she'd guess they were headed somewhere more remote than the capital.

"Don't be silly. Although—" she did her best to shape her lips into a pout "—when you told me to pack an overnight bag I did think it was possible I'd get a chance to see your apartment there. Or do you call it a love nest?"

Damned if she wasn't always surprising him. Every time he started to think of her as sweet and malleable, she drew a line, threw in a little spice and reminded him that she hadn't been referred to as the Ice Princess for nothing.

And he was glad. The occasional tartness of her tongue coupled with her refusal to worship at his feet pleased him. Immensely. "I can see I'm going to have to speak to Mrs. Siyadi. Sarab talks too much."

"Don't you dare."

"Very well. If you feel that strongly." He closed the space between them and cupped the back of her neck. "But I'm afraid my cooperation will come at a price."

She tipped her head up. "Blackmail, sheikh?"

He leaned down and lightly kissed one corner of her mouth. "I prefer to think of it as taking advantage of an irresistible opportunity."

"Lucky me." She turned her head and captured his lips with her own.

Their kiss was tender, teasing, full of mutual understanding and silent promises about the night to come. Kaj had never experienced a kiss quite like it, and while his body reacted predictably, his mind marveled. *This is what you've been waiting forever for. This closeness, this silent communion, this sense of rightness.*

Out of nowhere, unease slithered down his spine. Irritated, he brushed it away, telling himself it meant nothing, that it was simply the result of his lifelong habit of limiting whom he trusted. Given that he intended he and Catherine would be together for the rest of their lives, it was clearly time he started letting down a few barriers. As for the rest, they'd just have to see. Maybe with time…

He ran his hand down the silken valley of her spine. Urging her closer, he savored the slowly accelerating drumbeat of desire pounding through him. She was so very lovely. And he was so intent on exploring the sweetness of her mouth, it took him a moment to register that her hands were pressed against his shoulders, pushing him away.

He released her instantly. "Catherine? Sweetheart? What's the matter?" Even to his own ears, his voice sounded ragged.

She drew in a shaky breath of her own. "Nothing."

"Then why—"

"I have a surprise for you, too."

"Trust me." He reached for her. "Whatever it is, it can wait."

"It could, but that would also ruin it." She stepped back out of range.

"Catherine—"

"Indulge me, Kaj. Give me a minute and allow me to change into something more comfortable. Before I punch a hole through your carpets or break an ankle in these shoes."

"Take them off. Better yet, take everything off."

She smiled. "Try to be patient. Now, where did you put my bag?"

He took a firm grip on his temper and reminded himself that every woman he'd ever known had certain idiosyncrasies. If Catherine didn't want him to see her in her pantyhose, or something equally ridiculous, he supposed he could live with it. It wasn't as if he were some randy youth, after all; he was a grown man who for good reason prided himself on his self-control.

Still, he couldn't resist a small, long-suffering sigh. "Your bag is in the back of the tent, behind the partial wall."

"Thank you. You may not believe it now, but I think you'll appreciate the delay." Going up on tiptoe, she bussed his lips, then turned on the balls of her feet and headed inside.

Determined not to add to his own torture by watching the sway of her hips, Kaj resolutely turned away. Yet he couldn't seem to get Catherine's "surprise" completely out of his mind. What could she possibly have planned that was worth delaying their mutual satisfaction?

Clasping his hands behind his back, he walked over to where the supplies were stacked and made sure everything was in order. Next he checked the horses, who, unlike some people, seemed to welcome his company. Finally he walked back to the entrance to the pavilion and, desperate for a diversion, raised his face to the clear night sky and began to count stars, alternating between Arabic, French and English in a last-ditch attempt to keep from turning and walking inside.

Wahid, deux, three, *arba, cinq,* six...

He'd gone all the way to *sitten*—sixty—when Catherine's soft voice saved him. "Kaj?"

He turned. And looked. And looked some more.

Gone was his modern, sophisticated princess. In her place was a barefoot siren in diaphanous emerald-green trousers that clung to her hips and a matching jeweled bra that appeared to be at least one size too small for her full, high breasts. Her sleek, pale midriff was bare, exposing the shallow indentation of her navel. In sharp contrast, her hair and face were modestly veiled, leaving visible only her kohl-rimmed eyes, the lashes demurely downcast.

"Allah save me." He fell silent, forced to swallow

as he discovered there was no moisture left in his mouth. "Where did you get that outfit?"

"Mrs. Siyadi. According to her, Sarab's mother once flirted with the idea of being a dancer."

"You're not serious."

"I am."

"What about you? Do you also have aspirations to dance?"

"Oh, no. I thought we might explore more of the pleasures we shared last night. That is, if the idea pleases you...master." She finally lifted her eyes to him and he saw the hint of challenge in them, so at odds with the rest of her meek, harem girl mien.

It fired his blood the way nothing else could have. To his shock, he realized his hands were shaking. "Oh, it pleases me, woman. It pleases me mightily."

"Good." She closed her hand around his. "Then come."

He didn't require much urging. His breath was already labored, his body hot, tight and ready.

He let her lead him under the tent awning to the mattress. He reached for the buttons of his shirt, but when she brushed his hands away he allowed her to undress him. He even managed to keep his hands to himself when she stepped back to look at him in all his naked glory.

"I didn't know," she said softly, her gaze once more demurely downcast.

"What?"

As light as a feather, she traced a line from his throat to his navel with her finger. "That a man could be so beautiful."

He closed his hand around his erection, already so hard he almost hurt. "Even here?"

She reached out and nudged his hand away, replacing it with her own. "Especially here."

She gripped him, too gently. He parted his lips to tell her so, only to shudder with an overload of sensation as she tightened her hand and stroked her thumb over the broad, swollen tip of him.

It was clearly time to take control. Before she did him in.

He carefully unclasped her hand, eased down onto the mattress and stretched out on his back. Looking up, he held out his hand. "Come here."

"Do you want me to undress?"

"No." Executing an effortless stomach curl, he came up, caught her around the waist and pulled her down so she was straddling his lap. "Not yet. Or rather—" he reached around and deftly unfastened her glittering top "—not completely."

Her breasts spilled free as he tossed the jeweled fabric away. With a groan of pleasure, he cupped the soft, firm globes in his hands, then rubbed his smoothly shaven cheek over one taut, supple nipple. "Ah, but you're perfect. So soft. So very soft."

Sinking back, he propped his head on a pillow. He tugged her forward and down, pushed her face veil out of his way and began to suckle, first lightly licking just the tip of her nipple, then sucking gently, then working the erect bud with his teeth, carefully increasing the pressure until she began to rock against him in a tight little circle, chasing release. "Kaj—"

"Shh. There's no reason to hurry." He turned his head to her other breast, filled with an almost primitive satisfaction as he found that nipple already swollen and tender, just waiting for his mouth.

Catherine whimpered. What he was doing felt so very, very good, yet at the same time with every tug of his mouth she felt a growing tension. Pressing against him, she felt her warm center become slick with need.

With a faint smacking sound, he released her breast, gently gripped her shoulders and eased her up. "Such beautiful eyes you have, princess," he murmured, his thumb coming up to touch the corner of one above her veil. "Do you have any idea how exotic you look with your bare breasts and your veiled face?"

She shook her head.

"Well, you do." His hand dropped away from her face and he slid his warm palms beneath her arms. His thumbs brushed her nipples, then his hands drifted down even further, coming to rest just above the feminine swell of her hips. She held her breath as he spread his right hand and his thumb slowly stroked her silk-covered dampness. "No panties?"

She swallowed, feeling her pelvis begin to sway as the throbbing inside her grew. "No." Her voice was a mere whisper.

There was no mistaking his satisfaction. Or that the heat pouring off his golden skin seemed to originate in his silver eyes. "Good." With carefully calculated strength, he gripped the flimsy fabric between his fingers and yanked, splitting open the trousers cleanly at the crotch.

"Kaj!"

Ignoring her startled protest, he took a long look at

the dark auburn curls now framed by the emerald silk. "Ah, Catherine, you're like a picture of paradise. Come to me, *chaton*. Come to me now."

Her throat too tight to speak, she nodded. Then she came up on her knees, moved him into position and sank slowly down, exulting in the way he filled her like a broadsword sliding into a sheath. Biting her lip in order to stay focused, she waited until he was buried in her as far as he could go. And then, guided by an instinct she didn't question, she rotated her hips.

Kaj's control snapped.

Clamping his hands around her waist, he dug his heels into the mattress, lifted her up, then guided her back down as he thrust.

The pleasure was intense. Arching her back, Catherine braced her hands on his thighs and closed her eyes. So intent was she, she barely noticed when he rasped, "I want to see you. I want to see you when your pleasure comes," and reached up and tugged the veils from her hair and face. Instead, her entire being was focused on the quickening inside her as he drove in and out, slowly picking up speed like the piston of some great steam engine.

Again and again, they rocked together. Then Catherine felt him stiffen, felt his hands spasm against her hips, heard the low choked sound of exultation coming from his lips. She felt the hot, wet surge of him inside her, and her own body answered, contracting around him and rocking in wave after wave of pleasure.

When the storm finally passed, she fell bonelessly against his heaving chest, fairly certain she'd never be able to move again.

It was a long time before either of them spoke.

"Have I told you you're incredible?" Kaj murmured.

His breath tickled her cheek. "Umm. I can't really remember." She stroked his hair with her fingers, feeling drowsy, peaceful, replete. "Have I told you that I love you?"

He went very still. A second later he rolled to his side, propped himself up on an elbow and gazed down at her. "Do you mean that?"

She gazed steadily back at him. "Yes."

Just for an instant there was something in his expression—a twinge of sadness, a flicker of regret?— and then it vanished, replaced by a look of absolute resolve. "Then make me the happiest man on earth. Say you'll marry me. Please, *habibi*."

Habibi. She knew the word meant beloved, and her heart lifted. It might not be the declaration of undying love she longed for, but it was early yet. And it was obvious he cared. Plus she couldn't imagine her life without him. "If I did say yes, when would you want the ceremony?"

He didn't hesitate. "Next week."

"What?"

"Why wait?" He clasped her hand in his and pressed it to his heart. "I'm not some callow schoolboy. I know my own mind and I want you to be my wife. Not next month or the month after that. And just so we're clear, there's still half a year before my father's deadline, so it's not that."

She looked into his eyes and he looked steadily back. "Marry me, Catherine."

The last of her resistance crumbled. "Yes. Yes, Kaj. I'd be honored to be your wife."

Ten

"**D**arling, you look exquisite," Emma Rosemere Connelly said to Catherine, her gaze sweeping approvingly over her niece's ice-pink ball gown with its strapless beaded top and full tulle skirt. She paused the barest instant. "Exactly as a Royal should."

Catherine smiled fondly at the older woman. "Compared to you, Aunt Emma, I feel like a child playing dress up. You look perfect, as always."

It was true. The former Altarian princess, who'd shocked her parents and the world more than three decades earlier when she'd renounced her title to marry an upstart American businessman, had the sort of classic beauty that was timeless. She also had impeccable taste. Tonight she was wearing an elegant, plum-colored Chanel gown that was the perfect complement to her dark-blond hair and willowy figure.

Framed in the entrance to the suite of rooms that were now always kept ready for her at the royal palace, she looked at least a decade younger than her sixty years.

"I realize I'm here early," Catherine said. "But I wanted to see you and Uncle Grant for at least a few minutes without half the kingdom in attendance."

"And I'm glad you did." Putting an arm around Catherine's slender shoulders, Emma drew her inside. "Grant should join us in a moment. He's on the phone with Elena, your cousin Brett's new bride." Motioning her niece toward one of a pair of chairs grouped cozily together in the lavish sitting room, Emma sat down on the other. "They've been trying to connect with each other for the past two days."

Catherine made a face. "It has been hectic, hasn't it? I keep telling myself I'll get some sleep after the wedding."

Emma laughed softly. "From the way your sheikh looks at you, I wouldn't count on *that*, darling. As for all this feverish activity, you have only yourself to blame. First you call out of the blue from Walburaq to announce you're getting married. Then you ask Grant to give you away. And *then* you reveal you intend to hold the ceremony in barely more than a week!"

Catherine did her best to look contrite. "I know, and I am sorry. But as I believe I've mentioned, Kaj was quite insistent."

"Yes, and from the little I've seen of him, he's a very persuasive man. I must say, he reminds me more than a little of my Grant."

Catherine's gaze met her aunt's and for a moment the years between them fell away and they were simply two women discussing the men they loved. "I can see how he might. And not because they both have black hair and gray eyes."

Emma shook her head. "I should say not. What they share is an air of command, coupled with an indefinable something that proclaims they're all man." Her voice softened. "Not to mention that way they have of looking at you as if you're the only woman in the world."

"Are you two ladies talking about how wonderful I am again?" Still dynamic and vigorous at sixty-five, Grant Connelly strode into the room, instantly making it seem half its previous size.

Emma gave her husband a chiding look. "Did I also mention a healthy ego?" she inquired.

Grant winked at Catherine. "Of course I have a healthy ego." Pouring himself a brandy from the sideboard, he walked over and sat down on the sofa across from them and stretched out his tuxedo-clad legs. He took a shallow sip of his drink. "It takes an exceptional man to catch and tame an Altarian princess."

"Really, Grant," Emma protested. "You make Catherine and me sound like bucking broncos."

"Never, sweetheart." Grant's eyes twinkled. "I was thinking more along the lines of Thoroughbred mares. Spirited, headstrong and totally without equal. As I believe I mentioned to Catherine's young man at lunch today, he's marrying into exceptional stock. Just look at us. Thirty-five years and eight children later and I still think you're the most beautiful woman on earth."

His wife's smooth cheeks flushed with pleasure. Yet as Catherine knew, Altarian princesses of the old school had been raised to observe a very strict protocol, one that didn't allow for making intimate conversation with a man in public—even if that man was one's husband.

True to form, her aunt demurely changed the subject. "How was Elena?" she asked Grant. "Is she still feeling well?"

"Yes. Except for a slight case of exasperation. She claims that by the time the baby comes, Brett will have cornered the market on childbirth books and infant supplies."

Emma smiled. "Good for him. I hope you told her to take it easy."

"I did."

"And?" There was a brief silence as the two locked gazes. Finally, sounding faintly vexed, Emma elaborated. "Did she learn anything more about Ms. Donahue?"

Grant's expression abruptly sobered. "I'm sure Catherine has better things to concern herself with than our family problems, Em."

"Nonsense," his wife replied. "I know she'll want to hear about this since it concerns Seth. The two of them have always been particular friends. Haven't you, dear?" She glanced at her niece for confirmation.

"Yes, we have." And for good reason, Catherine thought. Seth was the third Connelly son, but he wasn't Emma's child; he was the product of a brief affair Grant had had early in his and Emma's marriage, when the conflicting styles of his driving ambition and her royal upbringing had resulted in a short separation.

Like Catherine, Seth had also been given up by his mother. And though he hadn't come to live with the Connellys until he was twelve and Catherine just four, an unlikely but very real bond had formed between the two cousins.

"So what did Elena say?" Emma asked.

Grant gave his snifter another swirl. "She finally managed to locate Angie and talk to her. Angie," he added for Catherine's benefit, "is Seth's biological mother. And though Elena didn't say so straight out, it's obvious she has some misgivings about her. Apparently, not only did the background check Elena did on Angie turn out too good to be true—Elena's words, not mine—but when they talked, Angie reportedly told Elena more than once how much she now regrets giving up Seth to us."

Emma's spine straightened. "You're not serious," she said, not even trying to hide her disbelief.

"I am."

"Well." For a moment Emma simply sat there. Then she lifted her chin just a fraction and said with obvious conviction, "Let us hope, for Seth's sake, that she's sincere."

"Yes. Let's." Grant looked at his wife with obvious admiration. "Have I mentioned lately how lucky I am to have you, Emma?" he said softly.

Emma Rosemere Connelly smiled at him, and for a moment they might have been alone, so thoroughly absorbed did they appear to be with each other.

And then Altaria's former princess seemed to remember who and where she was. She turned toward

Catherine. "Now, enough Connelly family drama," she said briskly. "Let's talk about you, darling. After all, that's why we're here."

"Your aunt's one hundred percent right," Grant chimed in. "I like your sheikh, but I can't say I'm wild about this hurried-up affair. You're not going to give me a grandniece or nephew in eight months, are you?"

"Uncle Grant!" Catherine protested.

He looked at her indignant face and chuckled. "Well, somebody had to ask."

There was a solid knock on the door. "I'll get it," Catherine announced, springing up and hurrying toward the entry. Briefly pressing her hands to her warm cheeks in an attempt to cool them, she took a breath, then opened the door.

She gave a start of surprised relief. "Kaj! What on earth are you doing here?"

Her fiancé, looking tall and dashing in exquisitely tailored evening wear, gave her an appreciative, all-encompassing look. "I came up to escort you downstairs, and your maid said I'd find you here. And from the look on your face, I'd say my timing is perfect as usual."

"Happy?" Kaj asked her as he expertly navigated a path for them through the crush of other dancers.

Catherine gave her head a slight shake. "No. Not really."

As she'd imagined he might, he instantly raised an eyebrow. "Pardon me?"

The waltz they were doing was one of her favorites, a fast step-step-whirl done while revolving around the floor. She smiled at the way the skirt of her dress billowed around her as they danced. It gave her almost as much pleasure as the sight of the large square-cut emerald and diamond ring glittering on her finger.

But neither meant as much as the solid weight of Kaj's hand against her hip, or how safe and protected she felt being in his arms. "Happy is far too tame a word to describe how I feel. Ebullient? Ecstatic? Deliriously thrilled? None of those are exactly right, either, but they come closer."

His gaze skated over her. "How about exquisite?" he said, tightening his hold as they twirled toward the far end of the ballroom.

"If I'm exquisite, it's merely reflected glory from being close to you." The cool air from the open French doors washed over them and she gave a soft sigh of appreciation.

"Hardly. There isn't a man in this room tonight who doesn't envy me. And for excellent reason."

"Are there other men here?" she asked. "I hadn't noticed. While you...I've missed you the past few days," she said softly. "I wake up during the night and wish you were beside me."

He gave her an indecipherable look. Then to her surprise, he abruptly altered course and danced them right out through the doors and onto the terrace.

She gave a gasp of laughter. "Kaj!"

"Hush. I wanted to do this that first time we danced, but controlled myself. I'm not about to give up a second opportunity." Without missing a beat, he led the way around a corner and backed her up against a short section of balustrade hidden by an enormous planter. "You're a menace to my peace of mind. You know that, don't you?" Pulling her flush against him, he found her mouth with his own.

Their kiss was mutually hungry, fueled by the past several days of deprivation. Although they'd managed a few other stolen kisses, it seemed they'd only served to heighten their desire for each other. Now, tongues tangled, hands feverishly searching for any available patch of bare skin, they clung together, desperate to touch and taste.

When finally they eased apart, Kaj tipped his head back and blew out a frustrated breath. "Three more days until the wedding," he said with disgust. "We should have eloped."

"I know." Smoothing her hands over the back of his jacket, Catherine rested her cheek against his black satin lapel. "Sometimes I don't think I can wait, either."

His concern immediately shifted to her. "Just how are you holding up to all this craziness? Every time I call you on the phone, that tyrant of a palace operator says, 'I'm sorry, sir, the princess is unavailable.'"

He sounded so insulted she had to smile. "I'm fine. Between Erin doing all the planning for tonight and Aunt Emma arranging the wedding, all I've had to do is say yes or no when they've asked my opinion. Although it's time consuming—"

"That's an understatement," Kaj muttered into her hair.

"—everything has gone far more smoothly than I expected. Except for missing you. And being unable to show you and Daniel that e-mail..." Although she did her best to keep the regret out of her voice when she got to that last part, Kaj wasn't fooled.

"I've told you, it doesn't matter that the e-mail was erased. It's the connection you drew between it and the photograph at Alf Ahkbar that's important. And now that you've told Daniel about it, he'll pass it along to his investigators who'll be sure to look into it. You needn't worry about that."

"I know. It's just...sometimes it doesn't feel right that I should be so happy, while Father and Grandfather—" She broke off, chiding herself for being negative on such a special night. "I'm sorry."

As he so often did, Kaj seemed to understand perfectly. "There's a reason the old cliché Life Is for the Living is an old cliché," he said gently. "I know you and your father had your differences and that King Thomas wasn't terribly demonstrative, but I don't think either one of them would begrudge you a chance at personal happiness. Do you? Truly?"

"No. I suppose not."

"Good. Now come here and let me help you forget your troubles."

He didn't have to ask again. Linking her arms around his strong neck, she leaned against him, heat instantly rising through her as his firm, warm lips moved over hers. Kissing him was better than drinking the headiest champagne, she thought. It made her feel bold and brave, hopeful, incredibly alive. It made her believe that anything was possible....

When they finally came up for air, Kaj gave a raspy chuckle. "Sweet, sweet Catherine. I'm afraid we'd best go in...while I still can."

She sighed, reluctantly released her hold on him and stepped back. "I suppose you're right."

They took a moment to straighten their clothes. "Ready?" he murmured, reaching for her hand.

"Yes."

Hand in hand they strolled from their trysting place across the terrace and on inside. They'd barely cleared the door when a familiar male voice said, "Ah, there you are."

Materializing out of the throng, Grant Connelly smiled at them. "I've been looking for you, Catherine. Do you think I might steal my niece for this next dance, sheikh?"

"As much as I hate to give her up, I suppose I must," Kaj said with a gracious smile, "seeing as we're soon to be family. Speaking of which, I need to see if my cousin's finally arrived, anyway. He was catching a late flight in. So if you'll excuse me?" Giving Catherine's hand a brief kiss, he nodded at the other man and strode away.

Grant watched him go for a second, then turned to Catherine, held out his hand and gestured to the dance floor. "After you, Your Highness."

Her smile, which had been feeling slightly strained, became genuine. "Thank you, Mr. Connelly."

With the ease of years of training she went easily into his arms, gracefully following his lead as the music started up again. "I believe I owe you an apology, Catherine," Grant said seriously. "I didn't mean to insult you earlier. Or imply that I don't have the highest regard for your character—"

"No, Uncle, please. Not another word. I know you

were kidding and trying to look out for me. It's all right, truly. It's rather nice to know that you care.''

"Of course I do. You're a special young woman, my dear. I hope you know how proud your aunt and I are of you.''

Touched, Catherine squeezed his hand. "Thank you."

Comfortable with each other, they danced without speaking for several turns of the floor. "Did your aunt tell you about the twins?" Grant finally inquired.

"Drew and Brett? What about them?" Her twenty-seven-year-old cousins were the only twins she knew.

"No. Douglas and Chance Barnett. Soon to be Barnett Connelly."

She felt her eyes widen. "You and Aunt Emma are adopting?"

He smiled ruefully and shook his head. "No. Of course not. The boys—men, actually, I guess—are mine. They were conceived by a woman I knew in college, before I ever met your aunt. Their mother chose not to tell me she was expecting. Or to tell them my identity. At least not until she fell mortally ill, and by then they felt they were old enough to take care of themselves."

"Good heavens."

"Yes. Oddly enough, it was all the publicity about Daniel coming here, to Altaria, that made them decide they might like to get to know me and the rest of the family."

"I'm not sure what to say. It all seems sort of fantastic, like something out of a movie."

"I couldn't agree more. It's been hard on your

aunt—hard on us both, really. But the good news is from what I can see, in addition to having the Connelly good looks—'' that faint rueful smile flashed again ''—they're both hardworking and resourceful young men. Chance is a Navy SEAL and Douglas is a doctor. We're having a big party to welcome them to the family once Emma and I get home. Jennifer is taking care of everything.''

Jennifer was Emma's social secretary, a blond, pretty, single mother about Catherine's own age whom she'd liked very much the one time they'd met. ''Are Tobias and Miss Lilly going to be there?'' Grant's parents were two of her favorites.

''Yes, they are. For once they're actually interrupting their annual Palm Springs hiatus—can you believe it?''

She shook her head. ''I'm sorry I'll have to miss it.''

''Now, none of that. You'll have plenty of time to see everyone some other time,'' Grant said easily. ''While with any luck, you'll only get married once.''

Catherine smiled.

And then, out of all the myriad conversations floating around them, a laugh from overhead arrested her attention. Looking over her uncle's shoulder, she caught sight of Kaj and Joffrey standing upstairs on the balcony.

Pleasure exploded like champagne bubbles through her veins at the sight of her fiancé, and she had a sudden urge to be with him, to touch him and share her overwhelming happiness with him. It was all she could do to uphold her end of the conversation for the remainder of the dance, and she could only hope

the manners that had been drilled into her since birth
stood her in good stead as the music came to an end.

She hoped she thanked Grant for the dance, but she
couldn't be certain.

Then she dismissed the concern. And picking up
her skirts, she turned and headed for the stairs.

"They may be a tad on the formal side, but these
Altarians do know how to throw a party," Joffrey
said, gazing admiringly down at the crush below.
"This is quite the impressive affair."

"Don't forget the new king and queen are Ameri-
cans," Kaj said. "And in case it's somehow escaped
your notice, I happen to be quite fond of Altarians.
At least, one in particular."

"Yes, I know. I've been meaning to talk to you
about that."

Kaj groaned. "Spare me, Joff. I assure you I already know more than you ever will about the birds
and the bees, nor do I need you to lecture me on the
responsibilities of marriage. Particularly when you
yourself are in possession of neither a wife nor even
a significant other, as I believe they're called. As for
love, you don't have any more experience with it,
dearest Joffrey, than I do."

"One does not need to be a poet in order to understand great verse," the Englishman said with dignity.

Kaj made a deliberately rude noise. "Please. If I
remember correctly, your last prediction—something
to the effect that I'd have a difficult time making a
certain princess aware I was alive—didn't pan out."

The other man made a vague, dismissive gesture.

"One slight miscalculation hardly disqualifies me to speak my mind."

"One? In case it's slipped your mind, it is currently March 26, my ring is on the aforementioned princess's finger, and you'll simply have to take my word as a gentleman that I fulfilled the third requirement of our wager. Speaking of which, when should I expect to receive my new Renoir?"

Joff grimaced. "I've been wondering when you'd be ill-mannered enough to bring that up. And I can't help but point out that you're being incredibly short-sighted. That painting clearly belongs in my drawing room. You yourself are always saying how perfect it is for the space. Think about how much you'll miss seeing it there when you come to England to visit."

"I'll survive. We had a wager, I won, and now—" He narrowed his eyes as Joff's gaze drifted to something beyond him. Accustomed to Joff's tendency to try to distract him whenever his cousin felt he was on the verge of losing an argument, Kaj pretended not to notice when the other man stiffened in seeming alarm. "Now I expect you to pay up. Just as I haven't a doubt you'd be pressing me to ship you Tezhari if the tables were turned."

"Kaj, shut up."

Damned if Joffrey didn't sound genuinely distressed. He stared at his cousin curiously. Then, with a faint shrug, he turned to see for himself what, if anything, was causing Joff's odd behavior.

Catherine stood no more than ten feet away, her gaze riveted on him, her face whiter than his shirt.

He swore under his breath. "Would you excuse us, Joff?" he said, never taking his eyes off his betrothed.

"Certainly."

He felt Joff withdraw. And then it was just Catherine and him.

This, Catherine thought, as she stood frozen in place, must be what it felt like to be struck by lightning.

She could hear the blood rushing through her ears, feel her pulse pounding, taste the metallic flavor of crushing hurt on her tongue. Her skin burned, but at her core she felt colder than death.

As for her heart... She couldn't feel it at all.

"Catherine, don't look like that," Kaj said sharply. Striding close, he reached out and clasped her cold hands in his own. "I'm sorry you had to hear that, but I assure you it meant nothing."

"You—" She stopped and wet her lips, which felt bruised and stiff. "You and your cousin had a bet? About me? About us?"

"Yes. But I promise it was made well before I got to know you, and was nothing more than the sort of stupid posturing that men are prone to."

"I see." And she did. She believed he was telling the truth. Unfortunately, that wasn't what had her rooted in place, feeling as if she'd had her soul torn out. It was what he'd said so casually to Joffrey before the bet had even come up:

"As for love, you don't have any more experience with it, dearest Joffrey, than I do."

She took a deep breath, then swallowed, trying to dredge up the courage to ask what she was very much afraid she already knew the answer to. "Do you love me, Kaj?"

Just for an instant he seemed taken aback. Then his expression cleared. "I want to spend the rest of my life with you, Catherine," he said persuasively. "I want you to be my wife, the mother of my children—"

"That's not what I asked you. Do you love me?"

"I care for you more than I've ever cared—"

"So the answer is no."

"Catherine, sweetheart, you're not listening—"

She jerked her head up at that. "Oh, no, you're wrong, Sheikh al bin Russard. For the first time I really *am* listening. And I'm hearing what you're saying. Or perhaps to be accurate, what you're *not* saying.

"And it's not your fault. You told me right from the beginning that you intended to marry me. I was just foolish enough to delude myself that, like me, somewhere along the way you'd fallen in love." Somehow she managed a slight shrug. "I love you, Kaj. And because of that, and what we've shared, for the first time in my life I feel worthy to be loved."

She pulled her hands free of his, slipped the beautiful emerald and diamond engagement ring he'd given her off her finger and pressed it into his hand. "So while you might be willing to live in a loveless marriage, I'm not." She looked him straight in the eye. "As of now, this engagement is off."

Then, not giving him a chance to respond, she turned and walked away.

Eleven

"So, are you going to go after her? Or are you just going to stand up here all night like some sort of lovelorn statue?"

Joff's ultrapolite voice punched through Kaj's paralysis. Slowly, feeling not unlike he had when he was fifteen and a spooked stallion had tossed him to the ground and stomped on him, he turned and addressed his cousin. "Go to hell."

Whatever he saw in Kaj's face chased every trace of amusement from Joff's expression. "I very likely will. Someday. In the meantime, why don't you tell me what happened?"

"What do you think happened? Catherine overheard our conversation and decided she'd prefer not to marry me."

"Because of the bet?" Joffrey said in amazement.

"You can't be serious. I mean, it was obvious she was upset, but I was sure once you explained and assured her how much you love her—" He broke off, his eyes abruptly narrowing on Kaj's face. "You *did* tell her you love her, didn't you?"

Confronted with his cousin's probing gaze, Kaj set his jaw and looked away.

There was a thunderous silence. And then Joff said carefully, "Would you care to tell me why you didn't?"

For a moment Kaj considered just walking away. Only the knowledge that his cousin would hound him clear to Walburaq and beyond until he had an answer prompted him to reply. "Because I care for her too much to lie."

There was another silence. This one, however, was much shorter, shattered as it was by Joff's snort of disgust. "Bloody hell! If that's not the most ludicrous thing you've ever said, I don't know what is!"

Kaj stiffened. "Spare me, please. I find I'm not presently in the mood for your opinion."

"Fine. But at least let me ask you this—if you don't love her, why the big rush to get married?"

"I beg your pardon. Apparently you've had so much to drink you've already forgotten our wager."

"To hell with the wager. It had nothing to do with this wedding, and you know it. All you had to do was be engaged by month's end. So I'll ask again—why the hurry?"

"Does it really matter?"

"Yes."

"Then my answer is, I don't know," Kaj said impatiently. "I suppose I wanted to get it over with."

"Ah. This from a man who's been dodging every beautiful, intelligent, eminently suitable woman intent on tossing herself at his feet or any other body part for longer than I can count? A man who could have married any female he ever dated with just a snap of his fingers? Who in the past decade became so well-known for his avoidance of the altar that his own father felt he had to blackmail him into wedding to ensure the family bloodline?" He sniffed in the particularly contemptuous way that only the English could really pull off. "Sorry, old boy, but I don't buy it."

"Then that's your problem."

"Hardly."

"And just what's that supposed to mean?"

"Just that if you're any kind of man, you'll also consider your princess. Because it's obvious she loves you. Just as it's also obvious—at least to me—that for the first time in your entire always-in-control-of-yourself life, you're in love as well."

"Really? And on what do you base your conclusion, if I might be so bold as to ask?"

"That's easy. Every sense you possess has been engaged by her from the very start. I've never seen you so single-minded about a woman, much less feel free to be your real self the way you are with Catherine. Most telling, just being with her clearly makes you happy. And I think all of that is because you fell in love with her that very first night, in this very palace, on that dance floor down below, when you first held her in your arms."

"Are you finished?"

"No. I also think you're scared. Scared because for

some reason you think if you acknowledge your feelings, things will go sour. That Catherine will turn into a tease like your mother and you'll become like your father—jaded, selfish, embittered.''

"I believe I've heard more than enough. If you value our friendship at all, Joffrey, you'll drop this now."

"Very well. But my leaving isn't going to change anything. Whether you admit it or not, your feelings aren't going to vanish merely because you want them to. And by refusing to face them, by insisting on basing your life on your parents' past, you'll get none of the joy you so rightly deserve—only misery. And that *will* make you like your father.''

Back rigid, face set, Kaj refused to respond, simply stared at the other man until Joffrey gave a slight, regretful shake of his head and retreated. Then Kaj swiveled back around and resumed his unseeing contemplation of the ballroom below.

Joffrey was wrong, he thought mutinously. Dead wrong. He was not in love with Catherine. Nor was he afraid—of anything. And he was most certainly not worried that he would ever turn into someone as empty and cut-off from real life as his father.

Really? So why, for the first time in your life, does the thought of going home to Alf Ahkbar bring you absolutely no pleasure? And why does the mere thought of living out the rest of your years without seeing a certain smile, hearing a particular laugh, having the right to touch and watch out for one special individual leave the taste of ashes in your mouth? As if you just burned down the only bridge that ever mattered—or ever will?

The future suddenly seemed to stretch out before him like a barren wasteland.

Unable to stop himself, he slid his hand into his pocket and drew out the ring Catherine had returned to him. On her slim, graceful hand it had shone, full of life and brilliance. Now, without her warmth, her fire, her vibrancy to define it, it seemed dull and lifeless.

Just like his heart.

In that moment he knew that somehow, some way, no matter what it took, he had to get her back.

Catherine sat huddled on the edge of the mattress in the dark sanctuary of her bedroom. Although she couldn't seem to stop shivering, she felt too listless to bother with a cover for her bare arms and shoulders. In much the same way, she couldn't summon the energy to reach over and switch on the bedside lamp.

Soon, she promised herself. Soon, she would pull herself together. She'd stop this ridiculous shaking and turn on a light. She'd climb to her feet and make her way to the powder room, where she'd smooth her hair and retouch her makeup. Then she'd lift her chin, plaster a smile on her face, go back downstairs and find Daniel or Erin or Emma or Grant and inform them the wedding was off. Surely they would then make some sort of announcement. One that would preclude any but the vaguest of explanations.

Because while there would no doubt be endless speculation, despite her brave words to Kaj she didn't think she could survive the whole world knowing that he simply didn't love her.

If she didn't hurt so much, it would almost be funny. Consider: after years of believing there was something about her that prevented the people she loved from loving her back, Kaj hadn't even had to dupe her into believing he cared. She'd done a more than adequate job of deceiving herself.

She made a small hiccuping sound. To her horror, it sounded almost like a sob. Clenching her teeth, she choked back the emotion threatening to spill out. She was not going to cry. She was *not*.

A sharp rapping sound momentarily startled her from her misery. For a second she couldn't imagine what she was hearing. Then, as she realized someone was knocking on her sitting room door, she nearly gave way to panic. She wasn't ready to face anyone yet. Not her maid, not her family. She needed more time, time to lick her wounds, to gather the cloak of her composure around her.

As abruptly as the knocking had started, it stopped. She held her breath as she heard the doorknob briefly rattle, and then the distinct memory of herself turning the lock surfaced in her mind. She sagged in relief, only to jerk to her feet at the violent sound of splintering wood.

There was a sudden flash of light as a lamp in the other room was snapped on, and then the carpet-cushioned thud of a long-legged stride she would have recognized anywhere.

"Catherine?" Kaj stood in the doorway, outlined by the light behind him. She couldn't see his face.

She didn't want to. Nor did she care for him to see hers.

Not now. Not like this.

"That locked door was a signal, Sheikh al bin Russard. It indicated my profound desire to be alone." Miracle of miracles, her voice sounded deceptively strong, even if her stride was unsteady as she made her way toward the balcony doors. Hugging her arms to her chest, she stopped before the tall panes of glass and pretended to gaze out. "In plain words, I don't want to see you. So please go away." She shut her eyes, praying he'd do as she asked.

"You're shaking." It was a statement, not a question.

She managed a shrug. "It doesn't concern you."

"Catherine—"

"*Go away.*"

"What a stubborn woman you are."

Something marvelously soft and warm slid around her icy shoulders. With a start, she realized it was Kaj's evening jacket. And that he must be right behind her. She frantically reached down and fumbled for the door handle. If she could just get out onto the balcony she could escape—

Too late. Reaching around her, Kaj caught her gently by the arm and turned her around to face him. "No doubt that's one of the reasons I love you."

She stared blankly up at him, telling herself she couldn't possibly have heard him right. "I'm sorry. I must have misunderstood. What did you say?"

"I'm a fool, *chaton*. And a stubborn one, at that. I've spent so many years determined never to repeat my parents' mistakes that somewhere along the way I lost sight of the truth. I blamed love for the failure of their marriage. But the reality is that what they had wasn't love at all.

"I know that now. Because of you. Right from the start you made me feel more alive than I ever had. You challenged me, you beguiled me, you infuriated and moved me. Most of all, you made me want more. Of your temper and your laughter, your passion, your insight, your heart. For the first time ever, I want to share my life. With you. I love you.

"Marry me. Be my wife. I can't promise it will be perfect—nothing ever is. But I swear you'll never again doubt how much I love you. Please, Catherine. Give me another chance."

She searched his face, the strong lines and planes starkly illuminated by the moonlight pouring in. He looked unwaveringly back at her, his chin firm, the curve of his mouth resolute. But it was the sight of his eyes, usually so steady, so direct, so forceful, that stole her breath and mended her aching heart.

They were sheened with tears, filled with uncertainty, alight with hope. For the first time they were totally open to her, nothing hidden, nothing held back.

"Yes." She reached up and cupped his lean cheek in her hand. "Oh, yes."

His thick, inky lashes swept down for an instant as a shudder of relief went through him. Then he leaned down and captured her mouth with his, kissing her with a sweet tenderness that was totally new.

Catherine didn't know how long they stood there, holding each other, exchanging kisses. All she knew was that when the first flash of brilliant light filled the room, for a second she thought it was just a reflection of her happiness.

Then another blazing burst lit up the grounds outside, and they turned just in time to see a pinwheel of colored light explode above the very cliffs where they'd shared their first passionate embrace. Another barrage followed and then another and another until the entire sky was painted with shimmering fireworks.

"Oh, I had no idea! How beautiful," Catherine breathed.

"Not half so beautiful as you, *habibi*."

And with that Kaj took her left hand, pressed a kiss to her palm and slipped her ring back on her finger where it belonged.

Epilogue

Epilogue

The first bell began to peal as Catherine and Kaj stepped out of the ancient chapel where Rosemeres had been getting married for more than two centuries.

A cry went up from the waiting crowd. Old ladies wept, the working men removed their caps, children waved, matrons called out their blessings. Then more bells began to ring, until the chiming seemed to stretch the entire length of the Kingdom of Altaria.

It was, Catherine thought, a joyous sound as much as one of thanksgiving. But it didn't compare to the sweetness that filled her every time she looked up at the tall man beside her.

Her husband.

She supposed that to anyone else, this moment right now—with Kaj in his formal gray cutaway and her in her pearl-encrusted satin gown, her long sheer veil held in place with a tiara of diamonds and flowers, their hands clasping each other's—would seem like the perfect fairy-tale ending.

But not to her. She knew this was just the beginning. That they had a whole life ahead of happily-ever-afters. And she couldn't wait to get started.

Kaj's fingers brushed her cheek. "Are you ready?"

"Yes. Absolutely."

He smiled. "Then let's go."

Her right hand held safely in his, she picked up her skirt with the other. Together they began the dash down the steps toward the waiting limousine, laughing as a shower of rose petals fell all around them.

*   *   *   *   *

DYNASTIES: THE CONNELLYS

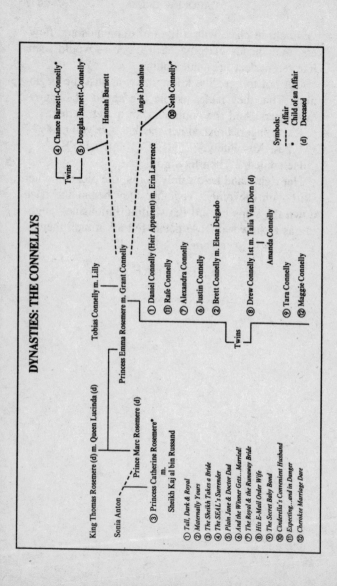

King Thomas Rosemere (d) m. Queen Lucinda (d)

Tobias Connelly m. Lilly

Princess Emma Rosemere m. Grant Connelly

Sonia Anton

Prince Marc Rosemere (d)

③ Princess Catherine Rosemere*
m.
Sheikh Kaj al bin Russand

Hannah Barnett

④ Chance Barnett-Connelly*
⑤ Douglas Barnett-Connelly*

Twins

Angie Donahue

⑳ Seth Connelly*

① Daniel Connelly (Heir Apparent) m. Erin Lawrence
⑪ Rafe Connelly
⑦ Alexandra Connelly
⑥ Justin Connelly
② Brett Connelly m. Elena Delgado
⑧ Drew Connelly 1st m. Talia Van Dorn (d)

Amanda Connelly

Twins

⑨ Tara Connelly
⑫ Maggie Connelly

① Tall, Dark & Royal
② Maternally Yours
③ The Sheikh Takes a Bride
④ The SEAL's Surrender
⑤ Plain Jane & Doctor Dad
⑥ And the Winner Gets...Married!
⑦ The Royal & the Runaway Bride
⑧ His E-Mail Order Wife
⑨ The Secret Baby Bond
⑩ Cinderella's Convenient Husband
⑪ Expecting...and in Danger
⑫ Cherokee Marriage Dare

Symbols:
- - - - Affair
• Child of an Affair
(d) Deceased

DYNASTIES: THE CONNELLYS
continues....

*Turn the page for a bonus look at
what's in store for you in the
next Connellys book
—only from Silhouette Desire.*

THE SEAL'S SURRENDER

by Maureen Child
April 2002

One

He hated parties.

Give Chance Barnett a machine gun, and he was a happy man. Tell him to mingle, and you got a mean dog on a short leash.

He clutched his beer bottle in a tight fist and made his way around the periphery of the party. His gaze narrowed slightly as he silently assessed his new family. A hell of a way to meet the relatives, he told himself. Yet he couldn't think of a better way to introduce himself and his twin, Douglas, to the rest of the Connellys. Though, to give them their due, they'd all taken the news of the twins' existence a lot easier than they might have. After all, it wasn't every day you met thirty-six-year-old illegitimate twins, was it?

Still, if he hadn't been wounded on his last mission, he'd have been happily out trooping through a jungle somewhere right now. And as soon as he was healed enough, that was just what he'd be doing, what he needed to do—get back to his SEAL team.

A SEAL in a Lake Shore mansion? Chance chuckled inwardly at the absurdity of it. His Navy whites were startling in a sea of bright colors and black tuxedos. But for the first time in his life, he was also in a room filled with people he was actually related to.

Weird.

He took a sip of beer, swallowed it and silently admitted that family wasn't necessarily a bad thing. It was just going to take some getting used to.

Still, he could do with some air.

Instinctively he moved toward the sliding glass doors that led onto a balcony. Conversation and piano music followed him as he skirted the crowd. But as he neared the glass partition, his plan for solitude fell apart.

A woman stood on the balcony, her short blond hair tousled by the wind. He knew her. Jennifer Anderson, Emma Connelly's social secretary. They'd met a couple of times in the past few days. She wasn't very tall, but every inch of her looked to be packed to perfection.

Her back was straight as she stared out at Lake Michigan, but he frowned as he noticed she kept one hand clasped across her mouth and couldn't quite hide the droop in her shoulders.

Instantly something inside him stirred to life. The protective instinct was strong, and he felt it push him outside.

"Get a grip, Jen," the woman muttered to herself before he had a chance to announce his presence.

"Crying's not going to help. It's only going to make you look like hell."

"Lady," he said softly, "all the tears in the world would have a hard time pulling that one off."

She turned quickly, her body language letting him know that she wasn't pleased at having been found giving in to tears. She recognized him right away.

"You surprised me," she said, lifting one hand to swipe away the telltale track of tears on her cheeks.

"Sorry," he said. "Old habits. I'm used to moving quietly."

"This isn't exactly the jungle, Commander." She turned away, deliberately ignoring him in the hopes that he'd go away.

Instead, he moved up right beside her.

"So," he said, "what seems to be the problem?"

"Problem?" She straightened up. The last thing she wanted or needed was sympathy. Especially from a man she didn't even know. Besides, he was a Connelly.

"Yeah," Chance said, sending her a glance, "when I see a beautiful woman, alone and crying on a balcony while there's a party going on not five feet from her...well, I naturally figure there's a problem."

She forced a cheer she didn't feel into her voice. "Thanks for asking, but I'm fine. Really."

"Yeah, I can see that."

She looked at him from the corner of her eye. "You don't believe me."

"Nope."

"Well," she said, pushing away from the balcony railing, "that's not my problem, is it?"

He reached out and grabbed her forearm. "Don't go."

His touch felt warm and strong and seemed to wrap itself not only around her arm, but around her bruised heart, too. Jennifer stopped short and lifted her gaze to look into amber eyes the exact color of fine, aged brandy. Her heartbeat stuttered slightly.

"I have a motto," he said. "Telling your troubles to a stranger is like talking to yourself. Only you don't have to answer your own questions." He smiled and her stomach flipped over for a moment.

But then, a cold, empty well opened up inside her and she felt her heart slide into it.

"Hey," he said, letting his hand slide from her forearm up to her shoulder. "I'm a SEAL. Trained to be a hero. So let me ride to the rescue here, okay?"

Jennifer looked closely at him. His brown hair was military short, but there was a slight wave to it that made a woman want to stroke her fingers through it. And good Lord, he was tall. With shoulders broad enough to balance the whole world.

Chance Burnett Connelly was handsome. Probably too handsome.

And right now, definitely too tempting…

* * * * *

Silhouette® Desire®

presents

DYNASTIES: THE CONNELLYS

A brand-new miniseries about the Connellys of Chicago, a wealthy, powerful American family tied by blood to the royal family of the island kingdom of Altaria. They're wealthy, powerful and rocked by scandal, betrayal…and passion!

Look for a whole year of glamorous and utterly romantic tales in 2002:

January: **TALL, DARK & ROYAL** by Leanne Banks

February: **MATERNALLY YOURS** by Kathie DeNosky

March: **THE SHEIKH TAKES A BRIDE** by Caroline Cross

April: **THE SEAL'S SURRENDER** by Maureen Child

May: **PLAIN JANE & DOCTOR DAD** by Kate Little

June: **AND THE WINNER GETS…MARRIED!** by Metsy Hingle

July: **THE ROYAL & THE RUNAWAY BRIDE** by Kathryn Jensen

August: **HIS E-MAIL ORDER WIFE** by Kristi Gold

September: **THE SECRET BABY BOND** by Cindy Gerard

October: **CINDERELLA'S CONVENIENT HUSBAND**
by Katherine Garbera

November: **EXPECTING…AND IN DANGER** by Eileen Wilks

December: **CHEROKEE MARRIAGE DARE**
by Sheri WhiteFeather

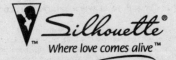

Silhouette®

Where love comes alive™

Visit Silhouette at www.eHarlequin.com

This Mother's Day Give Your Mom A Royal Treat

Win a fabulous one-week vacation in Puerto Rico for you and your mother at the luxurious Inter-Continental San Juan Resort & Casino. The prize includes round trip airfare for two, breakfast daily and a mother and daughter day of beauty at the beachfront hotel's spa.

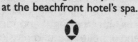

INTER·CONTINENTAL
San Juan
RESORT & CASINO

Here's all you have to do:

Tell us in 100 words or less how your mother helped with the romance in your life. It may be a story about your engagement, wedding or those boyfriends when you were a teenager or any other romantic advice from your mother. The entry will be judged based on its originality, emotionally compelling nature and sincerity.
See official rules on following page.

Send your entry to:
Mother's Day Contest

In Canada
P.O. Box 637
Fort Erie, Ontario
L2A 5X3

In U.S.A.
P.O. Box 9076
3010 Walden Ave.
Buffalo, NY
14269-9076

Or enter online at www.eHarlequin.com

All entries must be postmarked by April 1, 2002. Winner will be announced May 1, 2002. Contest open to Canadian and U.S. residents who are 18 years of age and older. No purchase necessary to enter. Void where prohibited.

PRROY

Silhouette® Desire.

Continues the captivating series from
bestselling author
BARBARA McCAULEY

SECRETS!

Hidden legacies, hidden loves—revel in the
unfolding of the Blackhawk siblings' deepest, most
desirable SECRETS!

Don't miss the next irresistible books in the series...

TAMING BLACKHAWK
On Sale May 2002
(SD #1437)

IN BLACKHAWK'S BED
On Sale July 2002
(SD #1447)

And look for another title on sale in 2003!

Available at your favorite retail outlet.

Silhouette®
Where love comes alive™

eHARLEQUIN.com

community | membership

buy books | authors | online reads | magazine | learn to write

buy books

Your one-stop shop for great reads at great prices. We have all your favorite Harlequin, Silhouette, MIRA and Steeple Hill books, as well as a host of other bestsellers in Other Romances. Discover a wide array of new releases, bargains and hard-to-find books today!

learn to write

Become the writer you always knew you could be: get tips and tools on how to craft the perfect romance novel and have your work critiqued by professional experts in romance fiction. Follow your dream now!

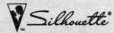

Silhouette®

Where love comes alive™—online...

SINTLTW

*Silhouette presents an exciting
new continuity series:*

**When a royal family rolls out the red carpet
for love, power and deception, will their
lives change forever?**

The saga begins in April 2002 with:

The Princess Is Pregnant!

by Laurie Paige (SE #1459)

**May: THE PRINCESS AND THE DUKE by Allison Leigh
(SE #1465)**

**June: ROYAL PROTOCOL by Christine Flynn
(SE #1471)**

Be sure to catch all nine Crown and Glory stories: the first three appear in
Silhouette Special Edition, the next three continue in Silhouette Romance
and the saga concludes with three books in Silhouette Desire.

―――――――――――――

And be sure not to miss more royal stories,
from Silhouette Intimate Moments'

Romancing
the Crown,

running January through December.